On Friday evening I was in my room. The door was locked as I didn't want anyone to catch me reading that article about European men.

Lorenzo DeGemma was about as handsome, sexy, and mysterious as anyone I'd ever seen, and I couldn't help imagining myself sitting in some café in Italy and meeting a younger version of him.

Up to that point in my life, the only boy who'd expressed any serious interest in me was Roy, who I was pretty sure was under some kind of spell cast by Heavenly. Roy was nice and sweet and a really good person and would have made a good boyfriend. But I had to be wary of him. After all, would you want him to be *your* boyfriend if you knew it hadn't really been his decision?

I glanced back down at the magazine again. What would it be like to meet an Italian boy with a deep tan and black hair and dark eyes?

From Archway Paperbacks

Here Comes Heavenly #1
Here Comes Heavenly #2: Dance Magic
Here Comes Heavenly #3: *Pastabilities*

Published by Pocket Books

From Minstrel Books

AGAINST THE ODDS™: Shark Bite
AGAINST THE ODDS™: Grizzly Attack
AGAINST THE ODDS™: Buzzard's Feast
AGAINST THE ODDS™: Gator Prey

Published by Pocket Books

HERE COMES HEAVENLY

PASTABILITIES

Todd Strasser

AN ARCHWAY PAPERBACK
Published by POCKET BOOKS
New York London Toronto Sydney Singapore

AN ARCHWAY PAPERBACK *Original*

An Archway Paperback published by
POCKET BOOKS, a division of Simon & Schuster Inc.
1230 Avenue of the Americas, New York, NY 10020

Copyright © 2000 by Todd Strasser

ISBN: 0-671-03628-9

First Archway Paperback printing February 2000

10 9 8 7 6 5 4 3 2 1

AN ARCHWAY PAPERBACK and colophon are registered trademarks of Simon & Schuster Inc.

Front cover illustration by Miro Sinovcic
Book design by Irva Mandelbaum

Printed in the U.S.A.

QB/X

IL 5+

to the next generation of pasta lovers—
Paulina, Carianne, Drew, and Jack

Chapter

1

"You can't hide your broccoli in your milk," said my twelve-year-old stepsister, Samara, at dinner.

"Shut up!" my ten-year-old brother, Robby, hissed back at her. "Maybe she won't notice."

The "she" he was talking about was the nanny, Heavenly Litebody. Robby had just slid a large piece of broccoli into his milk glass.

"I can see it," said my sixteen-year-old stepbrother, Chance, from across the table. "It's all green on this side of the glass."

Chance was Samara's brother. They were both Dad's kids. Robby and I, Kit Rand, were Mom's kids. Dad and Mom were both away on business trips as usual. Robby stuck his finger in the glass and moved the broccoli.

"How about now?" he asked.

1

"Can't see it," said Chance.

"But I can," I said.

"Okay, okay," Robby grumbled and stuck his finger into the glass again. "How about now?"

"No sign of it on this side," said Chance.

"Can't see it on this side, either," I said.

Robby sat back and crossed his arms. He gave Samara a triumphant smile. "See? You can *too* hide broccoli in milk."

"I still don't get it," Samara said. "You eat everything else, Robby. Why not broccoli?"

"Because I *hate* broccoli," Robby answered. "It's gross and disgusting and much too green. It's the one food I can't stand."

"Oh, yeah?" Chance raised an eyebrow. "What about sun-dried maggots?"

"What's a maggot?" asked Samara.

"The larva of a fly," Chance answered. "Like little white caterpillars."

"A baby fly?" Robby winced.

Chance nodded.

"That's so gross!" Samara wrinkled her nose.

"What's that got to do with eating?" I asked.

"They love 'em in China," Chance explained.

"To eat?" Robby stuck out his tongue and made a face.

"It's a good thing we live in Soundview Manor, not China," Samara said.

"For now," said Chance.

I stared across the table at him. Chance had brown hair and wonderful blue eyes. He was definitely one of the best-looking guys in Soundview, and even though he was my step-brother, meeting his gaze always gave me shivers.

"What do you mean, 'for now'?" I asked.

"Haven't you noticed?" Chance asked. "Mom and Dad have been totally stressed."

"They're always stressed," said Samara.

"Believe me, they're more stressed than usual," said Chance. "I hate to say this, but I think it's something big. One of those We-can't-tell-the-kids-till-we're-sure kind of things."

"Mom's having another baby!" Robby gasped.

"I don't think so," I said. "They don't spend enough time together for that to happen."

"Maybe they're getting divorced," said Robby.

"I don't think it's that, either," I said.

"Why not?" Robby asked.

"Same reason," I said. "They don't spend enough time together to want to get divorced. Chance, didn't you say something about China before?"

"Dad's been spending a lot of time there recently," Chance said. "And I thought I over-heard Mom and Dad talking about moving."

"To China?" Robby gasped.

"My guess would be Hong Kong," said Chance.

I stared at him. "Are you for real?"

Before Chance could answer, Tyler ran into the kitchen, followed by Heavenly.

Tyler was laughing as he ran. He was Mom and Dad's son. Heavenly was his newest nanny. Tyler was two years old and had short brown hair. Heavenly was probably in her mid-twenties and had spiky purple hair. Tyler didn't have a pierced belly button or a thin gold hoop through his eyebrow. Heavenly had both. Tyler didn't have any tattoos (yet). Heavenly had plenty. Tyler came from Mom. We weren't sure *where* Heavenly came from.

"Come back here, you scamp!" Heavenly laughed as Tyler raced around the kitchen table.

Bonk! Tyler banged into the back of my chair and fell down.

The rest of us watched in silence, waiting for the inevitable tears that followed one of Tyler's "crashes."

With a shocked expression on his face, Tyler slowly got to his feet. He wobbled unsteadily, then grinned. "Tyler fall down, go boom."

We all breathed a sigh of relief. Recently Tyler had started to run really fast. Unfortunately, his sense of direction wasn't very good.

"All feet and no brains," Chance said.

"That's not nice," I said.

"I'm not being mean," Chance explained. "It's just that he's at the point in life where his feet go a lot faster than his brain. That's why he keeps crashing into stuff."

Heavenly picked up Tyler and put him in his high chair and then glanced at the dinner table.

"Samara, you're the only one who didn't touch your broccoli," she said. We'd never met anyone like Heavenly before. She dressed wildly and did some very strange things, but she could also be really strict.

"So?" said Samara. "Robby didn't drink his milk."

Robby's eyes went wide!

"Drink your milk, Robby," Heavenly said.

"But—" Robby sputtered.

"No *buts*," Samara said with a sly smile as she picked up a piece of broccoli with her fork.

The phone started to ring. Everyone around the table traded looks, but no one got up to answer it.

"It's too early for Mom and Dad to be calling," said Robby.

"It's probably some girl calling for Chance," I said. Hardly a night went by that Chance didn't get five or six phone calls from girls.

"How do you know it's not Roy Chandler?" Chance asked back.

Roy Chandler was a boy I used to have a crush on. Then some funny stuff happened with Heavenly (funny stuff was always happening with Heavenly), and suddenly Roy had a big crush on me. The problem was, I was no longer sure how I felt about him.

The phone kept ringing.

"Isn't anyone going to answer it?" asked Samara.

"I will!" Robby jumped up. I think he was hoping that if he answered the phone, Heavenly might forget about the milk.

"Hello?" Robby said. "Oh, uh, she's right here." He held the phone to me.

"See?" Chance grinned. "I *told* you it was Roy."

"Wrong," said Robby. "It's a girl."

I took the phone. "Hello?"

"Kit, it's Jessica." I have to admit I was shocked. Jessica Huffington was pretty, blond, popular, and rich. She'd never paid attention to me until Heavenly arrived and "the funny stuff" began. Now she was always friendly in school. But this was the first time she'd ever called me.

"Hi, Jessica, what's up?" I said.

"The math homework. I really don't get it."

"Oh?" That sounded strange to me. I'd

always thought Jessica was pretty good at math. Not only that, but I was under the impression that she practically had a live-in tutor to help her with her homework.

"Have you done it yet?" she asked.

"I was going to start right after dinner," I said. "If you want, I could give you a call as soon as I look at it."

"Well, uh, since you haven't started it yet, maybe I could come over and we could do it together," Jessica suggested.

Jessica come here? This was getting weirder by the minute. Jessica was the kind of girl who expected *you* to come to *her*. I glanced over at Heavenly and checked to see if she was touching her left ear. She usually did that when she was making spells or magic or other funny stuff happen.

But Heavenly wasn't touching her left ear. And there weren't a lot of ladybugs around. That was another sign that funny stuff was going on.

"Kit? You still there?" Jessica asked on the phone.

"Oh, uh, sorry," I said.

"Maybe Chance could help us," she said.

Why Chance? I thought. He may have been two grades ahead of us, but he'd never been good in math and he was the last person in the world who'd want to help anyone with their homework. It wasn't that he was selfish or rude or anything like that. If you needed help in lacrosse or soccer, Chance would be happy to spend all day with you. But academics was definitely not his thing.

"Well, uh, I'm not so sure about Chance," I said. "But you're welcome to come over."

"He's there, isn't he?" Jessica asked.

"Yes."

"Great," Jessica said. "I'll be right over."

Chapter

2

I hung up the phone wondering what was going on. None of what just happened made any sense. But I didn't have time to think about it. Samara had just finished her broccoli.

"What about that milk?" Heavenly asked Robby.

"Actually, I'm not feeling so good," Robby said, propping his head up with his hands as if he didn't have the strength to sit up straight.

"What's wrong?" asked Heavenly.

"Maybe he's allergic to broccoli," Chance teased.

"Maybe you could shut your big mouth," Robby snapped.

"I hear that if you dip broccoli in milk, it makes all the allergies go away," Samara suggested snidely.

Heavenly stared at the glass in front of Robby.

"Uh-oh!" Chance whispered. "Busted!"

"It's only fair that if I have to eat my broccoli, Robby should have to drink his milk," Samara said with a smile.

Heavenly rubbed her chin. "Well, I can't say that I like to hear about young men who don't eat their broccoli."

Then she turned to Samara. "But what I *really* don't care for are tattletales."

As Heavenly spoke, she touched her left ear with her left hand. At almost the exact same moment I noticed a ladybug crawling across the kitchen table.

"If the rest of you are finished, please clean up the kitchen," Heavenly said. Then she turned to Tyler, who was sitting in his high chair. "All right, Mr. Wiggler, let's get you cleaned up and ready for bed."

"But what about Robby's milk?" Samara asked.

"Drink it, Robby," Heavenly said.

"But—" Robby started to protest.

"I said, drink it," Heavenly repeated firmly.

Robby let out a big sigh and picked up the glass. He slowly started to drink it. Samara watched with a smug look on her face. At first, Robby drank slowly, but as he drank more, he also drank faster. Finally, with a big grin on his face, he put down the empty glass.

And I mean *empty!*

Samara's eyes went wide. "Where's the broccoli?"

"What broccoli?" Robby replied with a smile.

"You know darn well what broccoli!" Samara cried. "The broccoli you hid in the milk because you didn't want to eat it!"

"I don't know what you're talking about," Robby said.

Samara turned to Chance and me. "*You* know!"

"I don't know what you're talking about either," I replied, trying to keep a straight face.

"Broccoli?" said Chance. "What broccoli?"

Samara's eyes began to fill with tears. She jumped up and ran out of the kitchen.

"Hey!" Robby said. "She's supposed to help clean up!"

"Let her go," I said. "She's having a bad night."

Heavenly took Tyler upstairs for a bath. Chance, Robby, and I started to clean up the kitchen.

"You really think we're gonna move?" Robby asked.

"I don't know," Chance said. "I guess we'll have to see when Mom and Dad get home from their trips."

"In the meantime, did anyone give the puppy dinner?" I asked as I cleared the table.

"What puppy?" Chance repeated as he scraped the dishes.

"Stormy, silly."

At the sound of his name, Stormy bounded into the kitchen. He now weighed close to forty pounds, and his fur was long and light reddish-blond-brown.

Woof! he barked playfully.

"You call *that* a puppy?" Chance asked while I poured dog food into Stormy's bowl.

"He's only six months old," I said. "He's supposed to get to be twice this size by the time he's full-grown."

"I can hardly wait," Chance groaned.

"Uh, guys?" Robby said as he loaded the dishwasher. "Did anyone besides me happen to notice that Heavenly made the broccoli disappear?"

"Gee, I thought you just swallowed that sucker whole," Chance said with a grin.

"I'm *serious!*" Robby insisted.

"We know, Robby," I said. "And we all *know* she can do stuff like that. The trouble is, we can't *prove* it."

"Maybe she's not allowed to talk about it," Robby speculated. "Like it's a Wicca rule or something."

Wiccans are a certain kind of sorceress who only use their magic for good. We were pretty sure Heavenly was a Wiccan or something like that.

Just then the front doorbell rang.

"That's Jessica," I said.

"Who?" Robby asked.

"Jessica 'Have It All' Huffington," I whispered.

"What does she want?" Robby asked.

"Help with her homework," I said.

Robby frowned. "She's never asked you for help with her homework before, has she?"

"Nope," I said as I dried my hands on a dish towel. "Guess there's a first time for everything."

Chapter

3

I went to the door and opened it. Jessica was standing outside.

"Hi!" she said brightly, and promptly gazed past me and into the house as if she was looking for something.

"Hi," I said. "Come on in."

Jessica came in and looked around. I couldn't help noticing how bouncy her blond hair was. It looked as if she'd just washed it. And she was wearing makeup and nice clothes. But then, Jessica always wore makeup and nice clothes.

"So, you want to go up to my room and do the math?" I asked.

"Uh . . ." Jessica hesitated. I watched as her eyes darted around. "Why don't we do it in the living room?"

"There isn't really a desk or table to write at."

"Oh, that's okay," Jessica said. "We can sit on the floor. I always sit on the floor when I do my homework at home."

Somehow I found it hard to imagine Jessica sitting on the floor doing anything. But I was trying to be a good host, so we went into the living room and settled down around the low glass coffee table. But we didn't start our homework. Instead, Jessica picked up a magazine. The headline on the cover said EUROPEAN MEN. Under the headline was a photo of a rakishly handsome bare-chested man wearing a pair of tight, worn-out jeans. He looked very sexy with his thumbs hooked through the belt loops of the jeans and an intense look in his eyes.

"Oh, look, it's Lorenzo DeGemma." Jessica started to thumb through the magazine.

"Who?" I asked.

"Just the biggest movie star in Italy," she explained.

"How come I've never heard of him?" I asked.

"Americans only like American movie stars," Jessica explained. "They're so provincial!"

"I guess that makes me pretty provincial, too," I observed.

"Oh, I didn't mean you, Kit," Jessica said quickly. "It's just that European men are so much more romantic than American men. I think Americans feel threatened by them."

"I wouldn't know." I opened my math book. "The only thing I feel threatened by right now is all the homework we have to do."

Jessica kept thumbing through the magazine. "Listen to this! It says that it is generally agreed that the most sensual men in Europe are the Italians."

"Very interesting," I said. "But I'm not sure it's going to help us get good grades in math."

Jessica rolled her eyes. "Really, Kit, you have to broaden your horizons. School isn't the only thing in life, you know."

"I know," I said, "but right now I'm a lot more worried about getting an incomplete on my math homework than about meeting a sexy, Italian man."

Just then Chance passed by on his way to the kitchen.

"Hi, Chance!" Jessica waved.

My stepbrother stopped. "Hey, Jessica, how's the pizza business?"

"Dad says we're just rolling in dough," Jessica replied with a grin.

"Glad to hear it." Chance started to turn away.

"Wait," Jessica said. "Could you help us with math?"

Chance frowned. "Well, I'd like to, but the way it works around here, Kit usually helps me with my homework."

He winked and left.

Jessica watched him go and sighed. "Talk about sexy. I wonder if your stepbrother has any Italian blood in him."

"Doubtful," I replied.

Jessica and I started to do our math homework. Jessica seemed to understand it perfectly and spent most of the time glancing at the doorway from the living room to the center hall of the house, as if waiting for Chance to come back.

Finally he did. He stopped in the doorway and looked in at us, which must have sent a thrill through Jessica.

"Hello, again." Jessica gave him her best smile.

"Need something?" I asked.

"A calculator," he said.

I pretended to be shocked. "You're not actually doing homework, are you?"

"No way." Chance grinned. "I just wanted to see what Bobby Platt's ten-year batting average was."

"Phew!" I pretended to be relieved. "For a second there you really scared me." I held up a black calculator. "I've got this one, but we're using it. Can I give it to you later?"

"Sure," Chance said. "I'll be upstairs."

He left. Jessica was still staring at the doorway after he'd gone.

"Hello?" I said.

She blinked and gave me a startled look. "Yes?"

I pointed down at our math book. "We were just about to do number seven."

"Does he *ever* do homework?" Jessica asked.

"Chance?" I shrugged. "Once in a while. If it's something he's interested in. He likes the war stuff in history. And anything that has to do with sports, of course. And sometimes he'll read a book."

"Interesting," Jessica said.

"Irresponsible is more like it," I said. "He's never going to get into a good college at this rate."

"My dad dropped out of college after one year," Jessica said. "He said he didn't need it for the pizza business. I guess he was right."

"Did he really start Huffy's Pizza by himself?" I asked.

"Yes," said Jessica. "He borrowed some money from my grandfather and opened his first shop. Then he opened another and another."

"How many Huffy's pizza shops are there now?" I asked.

"About three thousand," Jessica said, then added, "In this country. And another thousand around the world."

"Has he been to all of them?" I asked.

"Just about," Jessica said. "He travels a lot. This week he's in Brazil. They're opening a bunch of shops there."

Listening to Jessica talk about her father reminded me of what Chance had said about us maybe moving to China. Brazil sounded exciting. China sounded . . . far away.

We got back to work on our math and finished it.

"Well, that didn't take long," I said when we were done. "Seemed like you got it pretty fast."

"Sometimes it looks harder than it really is," Jessica replied as she closed her books. She glanced around. "This is such a neat house. Want to give me a tour?"

"Uh, sure." I got up. "Guess we'll start in the basement."

"Oh, don't bother," Jessica said. "Seen one basement, seen them all. Let's go upstairs."

"Fine with me." I stood up and picked up my books.

"Don't forget the calculator," Jessica said.

"Right."

We went up to the second floor. Jessica stopped outside a door with a sign on it that read:

THIS DOOR IS LOCKED.
PLEASE KNOCK AND WAIT.
DO NOT TOUCH THE DOORKNOB.
THANK YOU.

"What's this?" Jessica asked.

"Samara's room," I said. "She's a slug."

The next door we came to had a hand-written sign on a torn piece of loose-leaf notebook paper:

THIS DOOR IS UNLOCKED.
PLEASE BARGE IN.
FEEL FREE TO SPIT.
YOU'RE WELCOME.

We could hear rap music playing inside.

Jessica looked back at me. "Chance?"

"Who else?" I replied.

Jessica knocked.

"Can't you read?" Chance called from inside. "Just barge in."

Jessica giggled and pushed open the door. I knew I was going to enjoy what happened next.

Chapter

4

Jessica took half a step into Chance's room and then stopped and stared. I was pretty sure she'd never seen a room quite like it.

Chance was a collector of strange things, and his room was cluttered with all kinds of junk. In one corner was a wheel from a motorcycle. Against the wall was a surfboard with a big chunk missing. On his desk was a bent propeller from an outboard engine. The walls were covered with torn-out magazine ads for snowboards and surfboards and mountain bikes. On his bed were stacks of CDs, books, and magazines. Chance never slept in his bed. He preferred a thin mattress on the floor.

Recently, for reasons only he could explain, he'd hung olive-colored mosquito netting from the ceiling. It made his room look like the inside of a vagabond trader's tent out in the desert somewhere.

Now that we were inside his room, the rap music was louder. Chance was sitting at his computer, but he looked up as Jessica stepped into the room. "Can I help you?"

"Uh . . ." Jessica didn't seem to know what to say. I wasn't sure I'd ever seen her tongue-tied before.

"Uh . . ." Chance repeated with a smile. He always enjoyed shocking people.

"This room is really cool," Jessica said.

"You like it?" Chance asked with a teasing grin.

Jessica nodded. "It's . . . so different."

"Now, *there's* an understatement," I said with a smirk.

Jessica looked back at me as if she'd forgotten I was there. "The calculator," she said.

"Here you go." I tossed it across the room to Chance, who caught it.

"Thanks," said Chance.

"So what's with the rap music?" I asked.

"I like the words and what they say," Chance replied in a singsong way. "It reminds me of poetry in a way / The music's mad, but the beat is cool / And it sure beats studying for school."

"I'll remember that," I said and turned to Jessica. "Want to see the rest of the house?"

Chance was already busy with the calculator. The corners of Jessica's mouth turned down. I think she was disappointed that he seemed more interested in computing baseball averages than in her.

"Come on," I said. "Let's go to my room."

"Okay." Jessica followed me out of Chance's room, down the hall, and into my own bedroom.

"Ta-da!" I waved my arms around to show her my room. Not that there was anything special about it. I had some posters on the wall and shelves filled with books—nothing terribly interesting.

"Very nice," Jessica said unenthusiastically. It was obvious that my room wasn't where she wanted to be.

"So what do you want to do now?" I asked.

Jessica gave me an uncertain look. It wasn't hard to figure out what she was thinking.

"You want to know about Chance, right?" I said.

Jessica nodded and gave me a sheepish look. "Do you mind?"

Did I mind? Well, a little. But it had been obvious from the minute Jessica arrived that she hadn't come over for help with her math homework. She'd had other reasons, and most of them had to do with Chance.

I might have been surprised were it not for the fact that an average of five girls a night called him. If anything surprised me, it was that it had taken Jessica this long to notice Chance. How could I mind that yet another girl was interested?

"What do you want to know?" I asked.

"Is he . . . seeing anyone?" Jessica asked.

"Nope."

"Is there someone he wants to be seeing?"

"Not that I know of," I answered. "Then again, if there was, I'd probably be the last person he'd tell."

"He does like girls, doesn't he?" Jessica asked.

"As far as I know," I said.

Jessica bit her lip. "Do you think he'd like me?"

I raised my hands in the air and shrugged. "I wish I could tell you."

Jessica took a deep breath and let out a long sigh. "It's getting late. I guess I'd better go."

"Sure."

We went back downstairs. Jessica headed for the front door.

"Don't you have to call someone to come get you?" I asked.

"No, Spencer's waiting for me," Jessica said.

"Spencer?" I repeated as I punched in the

code that deactivated the alarm system. I pulled open the door. A shiny black car was parked in the driveway. A man wearing a dark suit and white shirt was sitting in the driver's seat, reading a newspaper.

"That's Spencer," Jessica said.

"You mean, he's a chauffeur?" I asked.

Jessica winced a little. "We don't like to use that word. We just say he's the family's driver."

"Right," I said.

Jessica dawdled by the door for a moment. "About Chance. Let's keep it a secret, okay?"

"You bet."

Jessica smiled. "Maybe you could drop a few hints? Like to see if he might like me?"

"Gotcha." I winked.

"Thanks, Kit." Jessica smiled. "You're a real pal."

She turned and went out to the black car.

What amazing nerve! I thought as I closed the door.

Chapter

5

I went back into the kitchen. Heavenly had put Tyler to bed and was now making our school lunches for the next day.

"She left?" Heavenly asked.

"Yup." I pulled open the freezer in search of ice cream.

"She didn't really want help with her homework, did she?" Heavenly asked.

"Nope."

"What did she want?"

"Chance," I said.

Heavenly gave me a sympathetic look. "That must make you mad."

"Not really," I answered as I took out a container of Fudge Rocky Road. "It's kind of what I'd expect from her."

"Well, at least you know what you're dealing with," Heavenly said.

"Yup." I finished scooping out the ice cream into a bowl and was about to put the container back in the refrigerator when the kitchen door opened and Chance came in.

"Where are you going with that Rocky Road?" he asked.

"Speak of the devil," said Heavenly.

"Where?" Chance stopped and pretended to look around.

"She meant you, silly," I said.

"What did I do now?" Chance asked as he got out a bowl.

"You were born charming, handsome, and altogether too much of a rascal," Heavenly said.

Chance grinned. "Hey, that sounds good."

"So what do you think of Jessica?" I asked.

"Who?" Chance replied as he scooped himself some ice cream.

"The pretty blond who was just in your room drooling over you," I said.

Chance shrugged. "There are a lot of babes in the world / Makes it hard to decide on just one girl / You may think you've found the girl of your dreams / But she's not as great as she first seems / The only answer is you have to hang loose / It sure beats hanging at the end of a noose."

"Bravo!" Heavenly laughed and clapped. "Master rapper Chance."

"Did you just make that up?" I asked.

Chance nodded sheepishly.

"Amazing," I said. "But you still haven't answered my question. What did you think of Jessica?"

"I'm not sure she's my type," Chance said.

"What is your type?" Heavenly asked.

"I don't know," said Chance.

"Then how do you know Jessica's not your type?" I asked.

Chance shrugged. "I bet you didn't know that Bobby Platt had a lifetime batting average of .382 with men in scoring position."

"Can't say that I did," I admitted, not bothering to add that I couldn't say I cared, either.

From outside came the sound of a car in the driveway.

"I bet that's your mom home from her trip," Heavenly said, getting up. "I'll get Samara and Robby. Why don't you two help her with her bags?"

Chance and I went out the front door. A taxi was backing out of the driveway, and Mom was pulling her black overnight bag up the walk. She was wearing a raincoat over her business clothes, even though it wasn't raining. Chance and I went out. Mom gave us both a hug and a kiss.

"I missed you both so much," she said. "How is everyone?"

"They're fine," I said. "You smell like airplanes. How was your trip?"

"Very interesting," Mom said. "Let's go inside and I'll tell you about it."

We went up the walk toward the house. I knew something unusual was going on. Mom went away on lots of business trips, and usually when you asked her how they'd gone, she'd just say she was glad to be home.

We went into the kitchen. Robby, Samara, and Heavenly were already there. Mom had to hug and kiss everyone, except Heavenly of course. Then she had to find out the latest news and whether there'd been any important phone calls. Then we all sat down at the kitchen table.

"I have some very exciting news," she said. "I've been offered a job in Italy."

The kitchen went silent. I'm not sure how Mom expected us to react.

"Why Italy?" Robby asked.

"Because that's where Telitalia has its headquarters," Mom explained.

"What's Telitalia?" Robby asked.

"A phone company," Mom answered.

"Moving there would be so cool!" Samara blurted. "Italy is awesome. They really know about style there."

"How do you know?" Chance asked.

"I read fashion magazines," Samara said. "Italy is one of the fashion capitals of the world. We'd know all the latest trends. We'd be way ahead of all our friends."

"Ya-hoo," Robby grumbled sarcastically.

"What about Parker Marks?" I asked. Parker was a boy Samara liked who lived over in Marwich. He was a young male model.

"He'll just have to wait for me," Samara said. One thing I had to say for my stepsister, she thought very highly of herself.

"Wait a minute," Chance said. "I'm confused, Mom. What happened to China?"

"China?" Mom frowned.

"Chance said he heard you and Dad talking about moving to China," I said.

"I *thought* that's what I heard," Chance stressed.

"Dad and I have talked about moving," Mom said. "And Dad has been in China recently. But that's not where we may move."

"You mean, we really may *move* to Italy?" Samara gasped.

"It's a possibility," said Mom. "I mean, provided that it's a good job and we all agree."

"But don't you know if it's a good job?" Robby asked.

"Not yet," Mom explained. "I know they

want me to be vice-president of the company, but I have to see what the company is like and meet with the people who work there first before I can decide if it's right for me."

"Could you be vice-president of the company and still live here?" Robby asked.

"No," Mom said. "If I took the job, I have to be in Italy. But there's no way I'm going without my family."

Chapter

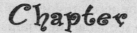 **6**

The next day at school I sat in the bleachers with my best friend, Darcy Shultz, during gym. She and I were on the same volleyball team, and we were resting while two other teams played. It was co-ed gym, and the teams were mixed boys and girls. But when we sat in the bleachers, we usually sat with those of our own sex.

"How does she do it?" Darcy asked.

"Who do what?" I asked sort of in a daze.

"Jessica," Darcy said.

"Huh?"

"Every other kid on her team has a red face and is sweating," Darcy said. "Their hair is all messed up. But Jessica looks perfect. Her hair is perfect. Even her gym clothes are perfect. How does she do it?"

"Watch," I said.

We both watched as Jessica carefully moved away from the ball every time it flew over the net.

"Amazing!" Darcy whispered.

"She's been doing it for years," I said.

"I always thought it took a lot of concentration *to get to* the ball," Darcy said with a smile. "But I never realized how hard it is to *stay away* from it!"

Darcy watched Jessica some more. I drifted off in thought again.

"By the way, I have more news about Shackelford and Litebody," Darcy said.

"Huh?" I wasn't following her.

"Remember I found that old photograph of that building and it said Shackelford and Litebody on it? And it was so weird because we always thought the Shackelfords started their company by themselves? And remember how we thought the Litebodys disappeared during the Depression? Well, I found out that they didn't really disappear. Only a few of them actually disappeared. The rest of the family stayed in Soundview Manor. But they lost all their money and had to live in a boardinghouse. . . . Kit?"

"Wha . . . ?" I blinked.

"Haven't you been listening?" Darcy asked.

"Sort of," I said.

"I thought you'd be really interested," she said.

"Well, I would," I said, "if there wasn't a good chance we were moving to Italy."

Darcy stared at me with wide eyes.

"My mom's been offered this job she's really interested in," I explained. "And the company's in Italy."

"But what about the rest of your family?" Darcy asked.

"I guess we all have to decide if we want to go," I said. "But if it's a really good job, I think it would be kind of selfish to keep her from taking it."

"And your dad's job?"

"Mom says he travels so much that it doesn't really matter where he lives," I said. "She says we could go to the American school in Rome and that it would be a great life adventure."

"And I'll lose my best friend," Darcy moped. "What will I do without you?"

For a moment Darcy and I sat with our chins in our hands and stared at the volleyball game in progress. There was nothing unusual about parents changing jobs and people moving. Even moving overseas wasn't so unusual. Just the year before a girl we really liked named Megan had moved with her family to London.

Out of the corner of my eye I noticed Darcy smile to herself.

"What is it?" I asked.

"You're going to think this is stupid, but did you see that article about European men?" she asked.

"The one about Italian men being voted the sexiest in the world?"

Darcy nodded. "I mean, it does sort of put a silver lining on it, doesn't it?"

I rolled my eyes. "Believe me, that's the last thing I'm thinking about right now."

"Do *you* want to go?" Darcy asked.

I shook my head. "Not really, but I keep thinking maybe Mom's right. Maybe it would be a once-in-a-lifetime opportunity."

"What about the puppy?" Darcy asked.

"Stormy can come with us," I said.

"I didn't mean Stormy, I meant Roy." Darcy nodded over at a group of boys sitting on the bleachers not far from us. Roy Chandler was in the group, but as usual, he was looking at me with puppy dog eyes. As soon as I caught his eye, he looked away.

"I don't think he can come with us," I said with a wink.

"What are you going to do about him?"

I shrugged. "Maybe it would be good for him. Maybe he'd forget about me."

"Don't count on it," Darcy said.

The gym teacher blew her whistle. Darcy stood up. "Come on. It's time for our team to play."

I got up and started down the bleachers toward the gym floor. At the same time Jessica's team was coming off. They were all red-faced and panting, except Jessica, who looked as if she'd just finished putting on makeup and brushing her hair.

"So, did you hear about Kit?" Darcy asked her. "She may be moving."

Jessica stopped and stared at me with a shocked expression. "Where?"

"Italy," I said.

Jessica's eyes went wide and her mouth fell open. "The whole family?"

"If we go," I said.

Darcy and I watched in amazement as Jessica's eyes began to glisten with tears. The next thing we knew, she ran across the gym and disappeared into the girls' locker room.

"What's with her?" Darcy asked.

"Chance," I said.

"Oh, no," Darcy said.

"Yup," I said. "Another one bites the dust."

"How do you know?" she asked.

The volleyball game began. In between points I told Darcy about Jessica coming over and pretending she needed help with her math homework when she really wanted to see Chance.

"Doesn't that make you mad?" Darcy asked.

"It would have if I believed that Jessica was a real friend," I said. "But who's kidding who?"

"I guess you're right," Darcy said. "Looks like this time Jessica 'Have It All' Huffington may not get what she wants after all."

I glanced back at the locker room doors. "I know this may sound strange, but I feel kind of bad for her. I mean, have you ever seen her get that upset over a boy?"

"No," Darcy admitted, "but knowing Jessica, it's bound to be a temporary setback. In a day or two she'll change her mind and decide she wants someone else."

I nodded in agreement. Little did I know how wrong we both were.

Chapter

7

Dad came back from his business trip to Hong Kong a few days later. I was eager to hear what he thought about moving to Italy, but we always had to wait a day or two for him to recover from jet lag and catch up with all his e-mail and other business at the office.

On Friday evening I was in my room. The door was locked as I didn't want anyone to catch me reading that article about European men. Lorenzo DeGemma was about as handsome, sexy, and mysterious as anyone I'd ever seen, and I couldn't help imagining myself sitting in some café in Italy and meeting a younger version of him.

Up to that point in my life, the only boy who'd expressed any serious interest in me was Roy, who I was pretty sure was under some kind of spell cast by Heavenly. Roy was nice and sweet and a really good person and would have made a good boyfriend. But I had to be wary of him. After all, would you want him to be *your* boyfriend if you knew it hadn't really been his decision?

I glanced back down at the magazine again. What would it be like to meet an Italian boy with a deep tan and black hair and dark eyes?

I was jolted from fantasy by Mom's voice over the intercom: "Everyone come down to the dining room for dinner."

I left my bedroom and found Robby and Chance in the upstairs hall.

"Did she say the dining room?" Robby asked in a low voice.

"That's what I thought she said," Chance replied. This was puzzling. The only times we ate in the dining room were birthdays, holidays or when we were having company over.

We went down to the dining room. The table was set with Mom's good plates and cloth napkins. Samara was already there, along with Tyler in his high chair. Heavenly came in from the kitchen carrying a basket filled with bread.

"What are you doing here?" I asked. I didn't say it in a mean way. It was just that Heavenly usually left on the weekends, as long as Mom or Dad was home to be with Tyler.

"Your mom asked me to stay for dinner tonight," Heavenly replied.

Chance, Robby, and I sat down. A moment later the doors from the kitchen swung open, and Mom and Dad came in carrying trays of food.

"Welcome to our Italian feast," Mom said cheerfully.

Everyone at the table shared a quiet look. The reason for this special dinner was suddenly obvious. Mom was trying to prepare us for Italy. But faced with our total lack of response, she paused and frowned.

"I thought you'd be delighted," she said.

"I am!" Samara blurted. "I think moving to Italy is going to be the coolest thing ever!"

Mom gazed at the rest of us. "You don't feel the same?"

No one said a word.

"Chance?" Dad said. "What about you?"

"I guess it'll be okay," my stepbrother said. "Soccer's pretty big over there."

"Robby?" Dad said next.

Robby shook his head. "I don't want to go. I like it here. This is where my friends are."

"But just think of all the wonderful Italian food you'll get to eat," Mom said.

"If I want Italian food, I can go to the pizzeria," Robby replied.

Dad turned to me. "How do you feel, Kit?"

The trouble with fantasies about handsome Italian boys is that they're . . . fantasies.

"Well, to be really honest, I think I'd be happier staying here in Soundview Manor," I said. "But I guess I should try to be more open-minded and say that I'd give it a chance."

"I think that's a very mature attitude on your part, Kit," Mom said. Then, with a disappointed expression on her face, she turned to Chance and Robby. "I was hoping you two would be more excited."

"Couldn't the people who want to go just go? And those who want to stay just stay?" Robby suggested. "I mean, it's not like we see a lot of you and Dad anyway."

Mom's face fell even further. Her eyes started to get watery.

"I really don't think that was the right thing to say, Robby," I said.

"The whole point is to try to keep the family together," Dad explained. "Not pull us even farther apart."

Mom turned to Heavenly. "What about you, Heavenly?"

"Go to Italy?" Heavenly said, surprised that she'd been asked. "I'd, er, guess so."

"Thank you." Mom nodded, then turned to the rest of us. "So the question is, what could we do to get Kit, Robby, and Chance more excited about the possibility of moving?"

"Maybe if we went for a visit first," Chance suggested. "Remember how I didn't want to go to sports camp the first time? And then we went up and saw the place and I got totally into it?"

Dad raised his head. "That's an excellent idea!"

"But when could we go?" Mom asked.

"Spring vacation's in a couple of weeks," I said.

"Interesting suggestion." Dad took out his hand-held computer. "I have to be in Germany the week before. Then I could fly down and join everyone in Rome."

Mom took out her hand-held computer. "I'll already be in Italy meeting with Telitalia. But Heavenly could bring the children over. And then we'd all be together."

"Great," Dad said. "It's settled. I'll call the travel agent. We'll all go to Italy on vacation and see how we like it."

I looked around the table to see how everyone reacted. Samara had a big smile on her face. Chance nodded approvingly. Robby crossed his arms stubbornly and stuck out his lower lip in a big pout to show that he wasn't happy at all.

But the strangest of all was Heavenly. She sat silently, looking wide-eyed and pale.

Chapter

I wanted to ask Heavenly what was wrong, but as soon as dinner ended, she left for the weekend. The rest of us spent the weekend around the house. On Sunday night Dad announced that the travel agent had gotten tickets for all of us and Heavenly to go to Italy over spring vacation. Mom called Wes Shackelford, our piano teacher, and arranged for him to take care of Stormy and our cat, Puff, while we were gone.

When I got to school on Monday, Roy was waiting at my locker for me. His hands were shoved deep into his pockets, and he had a pained look on his face.

"You're really moving to Italy?" he asked.

"Maybe," I said. "Nothing's been decided yet."

"Gee." Roy pursed his lips. "I—"

Before he could continue, Jessica joined us. "Did I hear a rumor that you're going to Rome for vacation to see whether you like it?" she asked.

"Yup," I said.

"Then you're not definitely moving?"

"Hard to say," I said.

"Do you know which hotel you'll be at?" she asked.

"Only that it's not far from the Trevi Fountain," I said. "And I think my dad said it was the hotel the prime minister of Great Britain always stayed in when he was in Rome."

"Sounds nice," Jessica said. "I hope you have a really fun trip. See ya."

Jessica headed off, leaving Roy and me alone again. Roy's shoulders were stooped, and he stared at the floor. I have to admit I felt totally awkward. Ever since Roy had developed his crush on me (with Heavenly's help), I could never be certain what he might do or say.

"Italy," he finally said.

"Yeah."

"Gee." Roy stared at the floor some more. This was so awkward it was almost painful. Finally I couldn't take it any longer.

"Roy?" I said.

"Yeah?" He raised his head and straightened up hopefully.

"I just wanted to say thanks," I said.

"Thanks?" Roy frowned.

"For being such a good friend."

"Friend?" Roy grimaced and hung his head.

I didn't know what to say or do. He looked so sad and disappointed. He reminded me of Stormy after we yelled at him for chewing up Dad's Birkenstocks. Suddenly I felt the impulse to kiss him . . . on the cheek, of course.

I started to lean forward.

Briiingg! Just as I did, the bell rang, and Roy lifted his head a little. "Kit?"

"Yes?" I stopped leaning forward.

"Do you think someday . . . something might change between us?"

I felt the impulse to play dumb. The problem was that I knew *exactly* what he was talking about.

"Maybe," I said.

"Really?" Roy lifted his head some more.

If only Heavenly hadn't put that spell on you, I thought a little sadly. "Yes."

Roy smiled broadly. With just those few words I'd filled his heart with hope again. I didn't know whether that was a good thing or not, but at least it got us out of that awkward situation.

Chapter

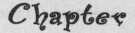

It was the night before we were supposed to go to Rome for vacation. Unfortunately, our plane didn't leave until seven P.M. the next evening, so that meant we still had one more day of school. Dad was in Germany, but the next day he would fly to Rome and meet us. Mom was already in Rome, meeting with the people from Telitalia.

Robby and I were setting the table for dinner when Tyler raced into the kitchen. A second later we heard a bark, and Stormy bounded into the kitchen and started to chase Tyler.

Tyler laughed and ran. He looked as if he was almost going to fall, but somehow he rarely did.

Robby and I watched Tyler run around and around the kitchen table with Stormy right

behind. Finally Tyler stumbled to a stop and sat
down on the kitchen floor. Stormy stopped next
to him and sat down.

They were both panting. Stormy's tongue
was hanging out. I was pretty sure that if Tyler's
tongue had been long enough, it would have
hung out, too.

"Tyler run fast!" Tyler announced proudly.

Woof! Stormy seemed to bark in agreement.

I noticed that Stormy's water bowl was
empty. So I filled it up and put it on the floor.
Stormy immediately started to lap up the water.
Then Tyler got on his hands and knees and
joined him!

"Gross!" Robby cried.

"Not for you, Tyler." I bent down and pulled
him away from the dog bowl.

"Yes!" Tyler insisted.

"No, you drink from a cup," I said, and tried
to give him a plastic cup of water.

"No, me dog!" Tyler said, pushing the cup of
water away. Robby and I shared a look. Then
Robby shrugged and filled a cereal bowl with
water and put it on the floor.

The next thing we knew, Tyler and Stormy
were shoulder to shoulder, both lapping up
water from bowls on the floor. Of course, that
had to be the precise moment that Heavenly
walked into the kitchen.

Usually I would have expected her to react in some way. Either to laugh at the sight, or maybe even be a little annoyed if she wasn't in a good mood. But Heavenly just stared silently and then went over to the oven to check on dinner.

Something was definitely not right. In fact, all through dinner Heavenly was uncharacteristically quiet. After dinner we cleaned the kitchen while Heavenly gave Tyler a bath before putting him to bed. As soon as we'd finished, I went upstairs. Usually when Heavenly was giving Tyler a bath, the nursery was filled with the sounds of laughter and splashing. But tonight it was quiet.

The door to the bathroom was open. As usual, Heavenly was kneeling beside the bathtub. Tyler was sitting in the bath. His wet hair was plastered down on his head and he was blowing bits of bubble bath foam off his hand.

"Seems kind of quiet in here," I said.

Heavenly looked over her shoulder at me. "Oh, hi, Kit."

"Heavenly sad," Tyler said.

"No, I'm not, silly willy." Heavenly picked up a handful of foam and put it on Tyler's head like a hat.

"You have been kind of quiet," I said.

"Sometimes I am," Heavenly said.

"I mean, for days."

Heavenly looked over her shoulder at me again.

"You want to tell me?" I asked.

"Have you got homework?" Heavenly asked back.

"Yes."

"Why don't you go to your room and do it," she suggested. "I'll come by once Tyler's tucked in."

I went to my room and got to work. It seemed like a long time passed before Heavenly finally showed up. I was sitting at my desk.

"Busy?" she asked from the doorway.

"It's under control," I said. "Come in."

Heavenly sat down on the bed.

"Don't you want to go on the trip?" I asked.

"Oh, yes." She nodded quickly. "I really do. It's not that."

"Then what is it?" I asked.

"Well . . ." Heavenly took a deep breath and let it out slowly. "If you want to know the truth, I've never been in an airplane."

I didn't know what to say. It was hard to believe. She had to be in her mid- to late twenties.

"Kit, please stop staring at me like I'm some kind of freak," Heavenly said. "Not everyone is as well-traveled as your family."

"Yes, I know, but you seem so . . . worldly," I said.

"I do?" Heavenly seemed surprised.

"I think so."

A small, crooked smile appeared on Heavenly's lips. "Well, I guess I should consider that a compliment."

I just gazed at her, completely puzzled.

"What is it?" Heavenly asked. "Am I the only person in the world who's nervous about flying?"

"It's not that," I said. "It's just that you look so hip and punk and you act so cool. I always assumed you'd . . . er, you know, been places."

Heavenly chuckled. "About the only places I've been are the insides of magazines and the Soundview Cineplex. But you can learn a lot from those things."

"But even if you haven't traveled that much," I said, "you'll be with us."

Heavenly sighed and looked away. I could tell it was still bothering her. It was so strange. Even though she looked wild and sometimes would do funny, crazy things with us, she also seemed very mature and grown-up. It was so hard to imagine that she'd be worried about something as common as flying.

"Listen," I said. "I'm sure you know that way, way more people get hurt each year in cars than in airplanes. I mean we learned in school that it's much, much more dangerous to drive than it is to fly."

Heavenly nodded. "I can't completely explain it, Kit. But don't worry. I'll be okay." She stood up. "I better get upstairs. I still haven't packed. See you in the morning."

Heavenly left my room. I barely had time to look down at my homework before someone knocked on my door.

"Come in," I called. Robby and Chance came in.

"Everything okay?" Chance asked.

"With what?" I asked back.

"Heavenly," Robby said. "After you left the kitchen, we started talking. You were right. She really has been acting weird lately."

"Guess who's never been in an airplane?" I said.

"For real?" Robby looked surprised.

"For real," I said. "And I think the whole idea has her freaked."

"Interesting," Chance said.

"Maybe she won't want to go!" Robby said hopefully. "And if she won't go, then we won't have to go!"

"I hate to say this, Robby," Chance said. "But the plane tickets are paid for, and Mom and Dad are looking forward to being with us."

"But it wouldn't be our fault," Robby said. "Or better yet, you and Kit and Samara could go and Heavenly could stay here with Tyler and me."

"Listen, Robby," I said. "I'm not so sure I want to go, either. But I think Mom and Dad expect to see all of us tomorrow in Rome. Now, why don't you go back to your room, okay? I need to talk to Chance about something."

Robby left. Chance fixed me with his piercing blue eyes. He always made me shiver when he did that.

"What do you think?" he asked.

"I think Heavenly seems really shaky about this whole thing," I said.

Chance shook his head as if he was a bit amazed. "Hard to believe."

"Do me a favor?" I asked. "Let's both come straight home after school tomorrow and make sure everything's okay."

Chance nodded. "I'll be here."

Chapter

10

The next morning when I got up, the familiar scent of breakfast was missing. The kitchen was empty. There was no sign that anyone had been there since the night before. I headed back upstairs.

"Where's Heavenly?" Robby was standing on the stairs, rubbing his sleepy eyes.

"Don't know," I said.

"That's weird. She's always up and making breakfast by the time we get up."

"Maybe she's not feeling well," I said. "I'm on my way up to see."

Farther up the stairs I met Samara coming down.

"Where are you going?" she asked.

"Heavenly's not in the kitchen," I said.

Samara frowned. "Who's going to make us breakfast?"

I just stared at her.

"What's with you?" she asked.

"Do you realize that until Heavenly came you never ate breakfast?" I said. "Now you can't live without it."

"I changed, okay?" Samara snorted.

"Amazing," I said and continued up the stairs. When you thought about it, it really was unreal how Heavenly had changed our lives. She wasn't like any nanny we'd ever had before. She really was more like a family member. On the second floor I went up the stairs that led to the third floor. Heavenly's door was closed. I stopped and knocked.

"Heavenly?"

No one answered. An awful thought shot through my mind. We'd had nannies who "vanished" before. They'd packed their bags in the middle of the night and simply left without saying goodbye. It was always a little upsetting when they did that, but they were usually nannies we didn't like anyway.

Heavenly, on the other hand, was the first nanny we all really liked. I knocked again. "Heavenly, if you don't answer I'm coming in."

No answer. I couldn't stand the suspense a second longer.

"Ready or not, here I come!" I pushed open the door. Heavenly's room was dim. The shades were drawn. Sheets and blankets were piled up on the bed. On the night table beside the bed was a paperback book called *The Idiot's Guide to Italian*. For a moment the room looked very empty. I felt a sharp intake of breath. Was she gone?

Then I noticed a foot sticking out from the pile of sheets and blankets. Several toes had silver toe rings. I let out a big sigh of relief.

"Heavenly?"

"Hmmmm." A sound came from the pile of sheets and blankets.

"It's time to get up," I said.

"It's time to go to bed," Heavenly groaned.

"It's morning," I said.

"I didn't sleep all night," she said.

"Is this about flying?" I asked.

"What else?" She yawned.

"I really don't get this," I said. "You're a grown-up. You take care of Tyler. You basically do all the mother stuff for Robby, Samara, Chance, and me. How can you be afraid of flying?"

"Easy."

"But everybody does it," I said.

"Not me," Heavenly replied from under the blankets.

"Didn't your parents ever take you on a vacation?"

"What parents?"

That caught me totally off guard. "You . . . don't have parents?"

"Nope."

"But you said you grew up here in Soundview."

"Yes."

"Without parents?"

"I was brought up by a lady named Cocci Nelliday."

"Coke-y? Like the soda?"

"She spelled it C-O-C-C-I," Heavenly said from under the blankets.

"What happened to your parents?" I asked.

"No one knows."

"How did this Cocci lady get involved?"

"I don't know," Heavenly answered. "She never told me. When I asked, she always said she was the right one to raise me."

"Just like you said you were the right one to be our nanny?"

"Correct."

Another clue in the mystery of Heavenly. I reminded myself to tell Darcy. "So where's Cocci now?"

The pile of blankets and sheets stirred and then rose up like a volcano getting ready to explode. But instead of a red-hot blast of molten lava, the only thing that popped out of the top was Heavenly's head. Her eyes were puffy and her purple hair was matted down around her ears.

"Guess I won't be getting any sleep." She yawned again.

"No, no!" I said. "You can go back to sleep. I'll make breakfast and get everyone off to school."

Heavenly frowned. "Then why did you come up here?"

"To make sure you were still here," I said.

"Where would I be if I wasn't here?" Heavenly asked.

"I don't know, but you weren't in the kitchen and I just wanted to make sure," I explained. "But really, if getting some more sleep will help you get ready for the trip, then you should do it."

Heavenly rolled her eyes. "Nothing could help me get ready for this trip. Besides, I'm amazed Tyler isn't up. I'd better go check on him."

Heavenly started to get out of bed, and I went back downstairs. By now Chance had joined Samara and Robby in the kitchen. They were drinking Mountain Dew and eating chocolate-chip cookies for breakfast.

"Wow, just like the old days," I said.

"Did you find Heavenly?" Samara asked.

"Yes."

"Why didn't she make breakfast?" Robby asked.

"She was having a hard time getting out of bed," I said. "She's totally weirded out about this trip. She's never been on a plane before."

"So is she gonna go or not?" Robby asked.

"You got me," I answered with a shrug.

Chapter

11

We were just leaving for school when Heavenly came down to the kitchen with Tyler. Heavenly's eyes were still puffy, and her hair was a mess. She didn't look happy when she saw that we'd had soda and cookies for breakfast, but she didn't say anything, either. She gave us all money to buy school lunches that day.

"So what's new?" Darcy asked at our regular lunch table that afternoon. "Feeling more excited about meeting all those handsome Italian men?"

It was funny that she'd asked. Even though it was a ridiculous fantasy, I didn't seem to be able to help myself. I was thinking about it, but I wasn't sure I wanted to admit it, even to my best friend.

"I guess," I answered, and then thought back to that morning. "Oh, listen, here's something you'll find interesting. Heavenly wasn't brought up by her parents. In fact, she never knew them and doesn't know what happened to them."

"Hmmm . . . a new twist," Darcy said.

"There's more," I said, then told her about Heavenly being raised by Cocci Nelliday.

"Never heard of her," Darcy said.

"Am I supposed to believe you've heard of everyone in this town?" I asked.

"No, but that's a pretty unusual name," Darcy said. "I'm definitely going to look into it."

Roy slid his tray onto the table beside me and joined us. The corners of his mouth were turned down. He gave me that sad, puppy dog look again. "How can you just move to Italy?"

"I told you it's not one hundred percent definite," I reminded him. "That's why we're taking this trip. To see if we like it."

"Everyone likes Italy," Roy moped. "My sister Janine says Italian men are the world's greatest lovers."

"Sounds like she read that article on European men," Darcy said with a wink.

We started to eat, and the conversation drifted into school matters. We were just finishing lunch when Jessica came by.

"Buon giorno!" she said. *"Come sta?"*

"What's that?" Roy asked.

"Sounds Italian to me," said Darcy.

"It means 'Good day. How are you?'" Jessica explained.

"What'd you do? Take instant Italian last night?" Roy asked.

"My mom and I have been taking Italian for years," Jessica said. "Just for fun."

Roy made a face. "Who takes a foreign language for fun?"

"Italy's one of our favorite countries," Jessica explained. "We go there all the time."

"All the time?" Darcy repeated with a raised eyebrow.

"At least once a year," Jessica explained.

"What a life." Roy sighed sadly and got up. "Guess I'll go play some ball."

Jessica, Darcy, and I watched him cross the cafeteria and go outside.

"He's really stuck on you," Darcy said.

"I know," I replied. "It's funny. When I had a crush on him, all I wanted was for him to pay attention to me. Now that he has a crush on me, I wish he'd pay less attention to me. I guess sometimes when your dreams come true, it's not quite what you expect."

"Well, that might be true of you," Jessica said. "But it definitely wouldn't happen to me if my dream came true."

"What's your dream?" Darcy asked.

"It's a secret," Jessica said, giving me a wink.

That's how I knew she was talking about Chance.

That afternoon I walked home from school with Samara and Robby. The high school had early dismissal that day so Chance would already be home.

"Just think!" Samara gushed. "Two hours from now we leave for the airport. Five hours from now we'll be on a plane headed for Rome!"

"Great," Robby grumbled. "Eight hours stuck in a little airplane seat, eating airplane food and listening to babies cry."

We got home. Chance was in the living room with Tyler, watching the big-screen TV. Normally Heavenly watched Tyler during the day, and we weren't supposed to watch TV.

"Where's Heavenly?" I asked.

"Upstairs," Chance said.

"Packing?" I guessed.

Chance gave me a funny look.

"Something's wrong?" I guessed.

"I got home from school," Chance said. "Heavenly was waiting inside the front door. She handed me Tyler and disappeared."

For the second time that day I took the stairs up to the third floor. Heavenly's door was closed and I knocked.

"Are you in there?" I called.

Heavenly didn't answer. I tried the door-knob, but the door was locked. In a way, that was good news.

"Okay, unless you climbed out the window, I'm assuming you're in there and you know that we're supposed to leave for the airport in a little while," I said.

Still no reply.

"Heavenly, millions of people fly every year," I said. "I told you before that it's the safest form of travel there is."

No answer. I felt stupid talking to the locked door. What if Heavenly wasn't even there? But where could she be otherwise?

"Heavenly, you have to come out," I said. "The plane tickets are paid for. Mom's already in Rome, and Dad's on his way from Germany. They'll totally freak if we don't meet them at the hotel."

I heard footsteps come up the stairs behind me. It was Robby.

"What's up?" he asked.

"She's locked herself in her room," I said.

"You mean, we may not have to go?" Robby cried with delight.

"Robby, we *have* to go," I said. "Mom and Dad will be waiting for us."

"But if Heavenly won't come, who's going to take us?" Robby asked.

It was a good question, and I didn't have a good answer. "Robby, what are you doing up here anyway?"

"Oh, uh, I just came up to say that Wes is here."

Wes, whose full name was Wesley Percifal Shackelford III, had offered to give us a ride to the airport.

Suddenly I had an idea and turned to Heavenly's locked door. "Did you hear that?" I said. "Wes is here. I'd hate to have to ask him to come up and talk to you."

Suddenly I began to hear rustling noises from the other side of the door. I smiled and winked at Robby. I had a feeling my plan was going to work!

Chapter

12

Ever since Heavenly arrived we'd known that Wes had a crush on her. You could tell because every time he was around her he'd start to stammer. It had always been hard to figure out how Heavenly felt about Wes, but I had an inkling that maybe she liked him a little, too.

I heard the lock on the other side of Heavenly's door click. A second later the door swung open, and Heavenly stood there looking very pale. The good news was that she was wearing hiking boots, jeans, and her bulky red sweater—her traveling clothes.

"I'll get you for this," she grumbled and started down the stairs past us, carrying her green backpack and *The Idiot's Guide to Italian*.

Robby gave me a disappointed look. "Does that mean we're going?"

"I think so." I started down the stairs.

Downstairs, I showed Wes how to take care of Stormy and Puff. By the time I'd finished, everyone's bags were lined up by the front door, along with Tyler's stroller. Everyone was dressed in their normal travel clothes except Samara, who was wearing a yellow dress, a straw hat, and sunglasses.

"What's with you?" Chance asked her.

"In Italy women dress formally," Samara said. "And they wear hats."

"What's with the sunglasses?" Robby asked.

"That's the way Italian movie starlets dress," I said.

Chance smirked. "So you think you're going to become an Italian movie starlet?"

"Maybe," Samara replied, sticking her nose in the air.

"Run, run!" Tyler raced out of the kitchen and into the living room doing his funny, off-balance run.

A moment later Heavenly appeared. "He's wearing me out. Would someone please get him?"

"Sure," Chance said. "Come on, Kit, we'll corner him."

With Chance and me coming from different sides, we managed to corner Tyler and capture him. A moment later we were back at the front door.

"So, uh, is everybody ready?" Wes asked, checking his watch.

"You bet!" Samara said eagerly.

"Then we'd better get the van loaded and go," said Wes. Besides teaching piano he was a disc jockey at parties and dances. He had a van he used to move his disc jockey equipment around in. It wasn't long before all our bags were packed inside.

"Passports and airplane tickets?" he asked as he closed the back doors of the van.

Everyone looked at Heavenly. She was supposed to bring that stuff.

"I think I have them," she said, a little bit uncertainly.

I gave her a look, but she averted her eyes.

"Maybe you ought to show us," I said.

"They're in my backpack, and it's in the back of the van," Heavenly said.

"If she says she has them," said Robby, "let's just go."

"No," I said. "I think we'd better check first. Just to make sure."

Wes got out of the van, opened the back doors, and pulled out Heavenly's backpack. We all waited while Heavenly opened the pack and searched around for the passports and airline tickets. Finally she pulled out a thick envelope. "Here they are!"

Samara turned to me. "Are you satisfied now?"

"Not quite," I replied.

"Why not?" Samara asked.

"Come on, Kit," said Chance. "Now what's the problem?"

I held out my hand. "Could I see the envelope?"

Heavenly hesitated. "Why?"

"Just curious," I said.

Heavenly reluctantly handed over the envelope. I opened it and went through the passports and tickets. I had to laugh.

"What's wrong?" Samara asked.

I gave Heavenly a knowing look. "Forget something?"

Heavenly narrowed her eyes at me and then headed back into the house.

"What'd she forget?" Chance asked.

"Her passport and ticket," I said.

"Serious?" Chance smiled.

I nodded.

"Wow," said Robby, "she really doesn't want to go."

Chapter

13

Heavenly sat in the front of the van on the way to the airport. At first she was really quiet, and I noticed that Wes kept glancing over at her with a concerned expression. Then slowly and gradually, they started to chat. Soon they were laughing and talking.

In the back, Chance leaned toward me. "Is it my imagination, or is Heavenly suddenly acting like everything's okay?"

"I think she's under a spell," I said in a low voice.

"You mean, from Wes?" Chance whispered.

"That's what I mean."

We got to the airport, and Wes helped us unload our bags and get Tyler into his stroller. Then he got back into the van. Heavenly watched him with a dreamy look on her face. I stepped close to her.

"Seems like things have warmed up between you two," I said.

Heavenly nodded and smiled.

"Well, we'll be back in eight days," I said.

As if the spell was suddenly broken, Heavenly looked around with a wide-eyed and somewhat fearful expression. I guess that was to be expected, since she'd never been in an airport before.

With Heavenly pushing Tyler's stroller and the rest of us pulling our bags, we went into the terminal.

"It's this way," Chance said, leading us to the international flights concourse. We got in a long line with a bunch of other passengers. The line wound around like a maze before it fed out at the ticket counter.

"Wow, this line is long," Chance said, checking his watch. "Good thing we have time to kill."

The line moved slowly, and we slowly dragged our bags with it. At one point I noticed Heavenly touching her left ear. That usually meant "funny stuff" was going to happen, but I didn't think much of it because we were in the middle of the airport.

We kept following the line around, pulling

our bags. I noticed a ladybug on one of the poles holding up the ropes that kept us in line, but I was too busy thinking about handsome, dark-haired Italian boys to be concerned with it.

"This line is taking forever," Robby complained after a while.

He was right. It really did seem to be taking a long time.

"I guess that's why they tell you to get to the airport two hours ahead of your flight," Chance said.

"How much time do we have?" Samara asked.

"About an hour and fifteen minutes," Chance said.

We kept dragging our bags around the line. After a while I noticed that all the people we'd been standing in line with were gone, and we were standing with a whole new group of people. That definitely seemed odd.

"I hate to say this," Samara said, "but I really feel like we're just going around in circles. How much time do we have now?"

"Forty-five minutes," Chance said.

"Maybe it's a plot," Robby said, using his ten-year-old imagination. "Like we'll stay in this line forever."

"That would be pretty funny," Chance said with a chuckle.

A plot . . . I thought. *Stay in line forever . . . And miss our flight . . . Wait a minute!*

I looked at Heavenly. She was gazing away as if she couldn't face me. Half a dozen ladybugs were crawling around our bags.

Stay in line forever . . .

"Heavenly?" I whispered.

"Huh?" Heavenly looked around at me.

"You're up to something," I said in a low voice.

"I am?" Heavenly replied innocently.

"With the line," I whispered. "Now, stop it."

She sighed and nodded. "Oh, okay."

She reached to her left ear. A few minutes later it was suddenly our turn to go to the counter.

"That was totally weird!" Robby said. "First it seemed like we weren't getting anywhere. Then the next thing you know, we're at the head of the line."

"Like magic," I said, shooting Heavenly a look.

Robby's eyes widened and he looked at Heavenly, too.

"Next, please," called a ticket agent behind the counter.

We went up to the counter and showed him our tickets and passports. We got our seating assignments and left our heavy bags. Next we got in line to go through the metal detectors. Heavenly suddenly stopped.

"What is this?" she asked nervously.

"Just metal detectors," I said. "Don't worry. They can't hurt you."

It took a moment to explain to Heavenly why we had to take Tyler out of the stroller and send the stroller on the conveyor belt through the X-ray machine, but she finally understood that we didn't intend to put Tyler through the X-ray machine.

Next we walked toward our gate. Heavenly stared at all the travelers waiting in the other gates for their planes. We got to our gate and sat down. Heavenly sat up straight in her chair and looked around, jumpy and wide-eyed. I'd never seen her act like that.

"I'm going to get some candy," Robby announced.

"And I want a magazine," said Samara.

They both started to get up. Heavenly looked as if she was going to say no.

"Don't worry," Samara said. "We're only going over there." She pointed across the concourse at a magazine and candy stand.

Heavenly seemed to calm down a little. I leaned close to her. "See all these people?" I whispered. "They've all taken planes a million times, and they're all still alive."

"Everything's going to be fine," Chance assured her.

Heavenly nodded. "I know. Just bear with me. And thanks for being patient."

Robby got some candy and a comic book. Samara got a fashion magazine. Chance plugged himself into his Discman, and Tyler took a nap in his stroller. We settled into the waiting-lounge seats. The minutes ticked past, and the waiting area became more and more crowded. People sat in the lounge and watched Airport CNN on TV.

While we waited, all the typical announcements came over the speakers. Warnings not to leave cars or bags unattended. Announcements of arrivals and departures. Boarding announcements. Everyone in my family had heard them lots of times. We hardly paid any attention to them.

But Heavenly listened carefully to each and every announcement. She was like a rabbit up on its haunches, ears pricked, watching, listening, even sniffing everything. Attuned to every little change.

When a ticket agent came around and opened the door to the Jetway, Heavenly quickly turned to me.

"Why did she do that?" she asked.

"It's nothing," I said. "It just means we're going to board soon."

It may have meant nothing to me, but it meant plenty to Heavenly. She went pale and then closed her eyes and reached for her left ear.

The phone on the gate ticket counter began to ring. One of the attendants answered it. I watched curiously as she spoke in a low voice. The lines in her forehead creased. She picked up the mike.

"Ladies and gentlemen waiting to board flight 422 to Rome, there's been a delay in, er, the food preparation department. Please be patient. We'll give you more information as soon as we can."

Chance was so into his music that he didn't even hear the announcement.

"That's a new one," Robby grumbled, and then looked back down at his comic book.

People in the waiting area began to frown and mutter to each other. *A delay in food preparation?* I'd never heard of such a thing. Meanwhile, I noticed a ladybug crawling along the armrest of my chair. Another crawled over Heavenly's backpack.

Heavenly opened her eyes. Her left hand was still touching her left ear. We stared at each other.

"I can't believe you did that," I whispered.

"Did what?" Heavenly asked innocently.

I touched my left ear and moved my lips in an imitation of what I'd seen her do. Then I pointed at the ladybugs. "A delay in food preparation? And ladybugs in an airport? Give me a break."

Heavenly glanced at the others. Tyler was still sleeping. Chance was still lost in his music, and Robby and Samara were engrossed in their reading. She looked back at me.

"I'm sorry, Kit, but I'm scared," she whispered.

"I told you, there's nothing to be scared of," I whispered back.

"It's easy for *you* to say," Heavenly said.

I waved my arm around the waiting room, which was now overflowing with unhappy-looking travelers. "You can't do this to all these people," I whispered. "It's not fair. They have a right to go on their trips."

Heavenly looked around at all the sad and upset faces. Then she closed her eyes and touched her ear. I noticed one of the ladybugs take off and fly away.

The phone on the counter rang, and the attendant answered it. A smile appeared on her face, and a moment later she picked up the mike. "Ladies and gentlemen, we will now begin boarding flight 422 to Rome. People traveling with small children, and others needing assistance, please go to the gate."

"Come on, that's us," I said, getting up.

Everyone got up. Chance pushed Tyler's stroller toward the gate, and I walked with Heavenly, who held my hand and squeezed so hard that it felt as if she was going to crush my fingers. I practically had to drag her down the Jetway to the airplane door.

Meanwhile, Chance packed up Tyler's stroller and stuck it in a closet inside the jet's door. He picked up Tyler and led the way into the back, followed by Samara, Robby, Heavenly, and me.

We passed through the first-class cabin with its big, wide seats, then through business class, and finally got to the coach seats. Suddenly Heavenly stopped.

"Now what's wrong?" I whispered behind her.

"Look at those seats," she whispered back. "They're so tiny."

"Welcome to coach," Samara muttered.

"How long is the flight to Rome?" Heavenly asked.

"Seven or eight hours, depending on how long we sit on the runway before takeoff," Robby answered.

"I can't sit in one of those seats for seven hours," Heavenly gasped. She pointed back at first class. "Why can't we sit in those seats?"

"Because that's first class, and it would cost a fortune for all six of us to sit there," Samara answered.

"Ahem!" A tall, bearded man behind us cleared his throat loudly. "Excuse me, but I'd like to get to my seat."

"Come on, Heavenly, we have to sit down," I said. "We can't just stand here blocking the aisle."

"I can't, I'm sorry, but I just can't," Heavenly muttered under her breath. She closed her eyes and reached for her left ear.

"Heavenly!" I hissed, trying to stop her before she caused another delay. She opened her eyes, then reached into her backpack and pulled out our plane tickets. "Look, I think they've made a mistake!"

"Oh, great!" grumbled the tall, bearded man behind us.

"What kind of mistake?" Chance asked. He took the tickets from her and studied them. "No way! We're in the first class!"

Chapter

14

Let me see those tickets!" Samara grabbed the tickets out of Chance's hand and squinted at them. "I can't believe it! Excuse me!" She started back up the aisle, squeezing past the tall, bearded man and the other people behind him. The rest of us followed.

"This is the most ridiculous thing I've ever heard!" grumbled the tall, bearded man. "How could you not know you were in first class?"

"Sorry," I said. "Our parents bought us the tickets. We just assumed we were in coach."

The grumbling of the passengers in the coach aisle was nothing compared to what was going on in the first-class cabin.

"I'm terribly sorry, Mr. Baxter," a flight attendant was saying to a short, thin, elegantly dressed man with blond hair, "but your ticket clearly says coach."

"That's preposterous!" Mr. Baxter sputtered. "I've never flown coach in my whole life!"

Similar conversations were going on with five other passengers who'd assumed they'd purchased first-class tickets and were now being told they had to fly coach.

After a great deal of argument and threats to sue the airline, Mr. Baxter and the other five passengers finally left the first-class cabin and went to sit in coach. I know some of you might think that what Heavenly did wasn't fair to those people who had the seats. Even I felt a twinge of guilt, but I knew that Heavenly would only do such a thing if she was really, *really* freaked about sitting in those coach seats. Anyway, the next thing I knew we Rands were reclining in our large, comfortable first-class seats.

"Check this out!" Chance made his seat go so far back he was practically lying down. At the same time a special footrest rose up to support his legs.

"And how about this?" Robby adjusted the small TV screen coming out of his armrest. "I can watch anything I want!"

"I'll have a Shirley Temple, please," Samara said to the flight attendant who asked us for a drink order even before the plane took off.

"Airplane!" Tyler, standing in the window seat next to Heavenly, pointed out the window at a plane at the gate next to us.

"Excuse me, ma'am," the flight attendant said to Heavenly, "but when we get ready for takeoff, he'll have to be strapped in."

"I understand," Heavenly replied with a smile. Sitting across the aisle from her, I leaned in her direction.

"Feeling better?" I asked.

Heavenly nodded.

"This is the life!" Chance said as he sat with his feet up, sipping a Coke.

"Yeah," said Robby. "I can't believe Mom and Dad sprang for first-class seats!"

"They didn't, dummy," Chance said with a smirk, and jerked his head at Heavenly.

"What?" Robby seemed surprised for a moment. "Oh, right."

The plane left the gate and taxied out to the runway. The only moment where I thought Heavenly might freak out was when we started to take off. The loud roar and thrust of the engines caught her by surprise and really scared her. Almost by reflex her left hand started to rise toward her left ear.

Luckily, I was sitting across the aisle to her left, and I managed to reach across and grab her hand before she could touch her ear. Who knows what she might have done to the airplane if I hadn't stopped her!

Heavenly gave me a surprised look, then let me hold her hand until we'd taken off, gained altitude, and leveled out high in the sky. I was dying to talk to her about the magic she'd used to change our seats, but she was busy keeping Tyler occupied.

Even in our wide, comfortable seats, with a special dinner and our own personal TVs, it was a long flight. Since it was overnight, the flight attendant turned off the cabin lights after a while. We slid the plastic window covers down and the first-class cabin became dark and quiet. One by one, the other members of my family turned off their TVs, tilted their seats back, and closed their eyes.

Finally, when I was pretty sure they were all asleep, I turned to Heavenly. I wasn't surprised that she was wide-eyed and awake, studying *The Idiot's Guide to Italian*. She may have been more relaxed than before, but she was nowhere near going to sleep.

"Tell me," I whispered.

Heavenly looked up from the book and glanced around. Except for some dim lights on the floor, the first-class cabin was almost completely dark. "What do you want to know?"

I felt a thrill. She was finally admitting it! "Well, how?"

"I touch my ear and wish," she said. "You've seen it."

"It can't be that simple," I whispered back. "I can touch my ear and wish, too, but nothing happens."

"You haven't been trained," Heavenly said.

"Who trained you?" I asked.

"Cocci."

"The lady who brought you up?"

Heavenly nodded.

I just stared at her. "I can't believe you're telling me this!"

"No," Heavenly whispered. "What you can't believe is that it can really happen. But that's okay. Neither could I at first."

"Is it Wicca?" I asked.

"Something like that. To tell you the truth, I'm not really sure. All I know is what Cocci taught me."

"Is Cocci still around?" I asked.

"Yes, she lives in town."

"Have I ever seen her?" I asked.

"Probably."

"What does she look like?"

"She has long straight brown hair that she parts in the middle, and she likes to wear big hoop earrings."

I tried to think. "I can't remember her."

"That's okay."

I was starting to feel tired, but I fought the desire to lean my head back and go to sleep. "Can I ask you another question?"

"Okay."

"I've always been curious about how you dress," I said.

"You're wondering if the tattoos and piercings have anything to do with my powers?" Heavenly asked.

I nodded. I felt a yawn coming and tried to stifle it, but I couldn't.

"It doesn't, really," Heavenly said. "Cocci says I've always dressed differently. She thinks it's because I know I'm different. I just like it."

Except for the steady hum of the jet engines, the cabin was quiet. My eyes were getting heavy. I pushed my seat back and brought up the footrest. I guess I must've been tired, because I couldn't think of anything more to ask. I just kept thinking, *I can't believe this! I just can't believe this!*

Then I must have fallen asleep.

Chapter

15

The next time I was really awake was when the airplane captain announced that we would soon be landing at Leonardo DaVinci Airport. In the seat to my left Samara slid open the plastic window shade. Sunlight streamed into the first-class cabin, and we squinted as we looked outside. The plane was descending through the clouds. Below us were fields. Some were green. Others were brown or tan. It looked like farmland.

To my right, Heavenly looked worried again. I held her hand until we'd landed.

The airport was modern, glassy, and busy. We got our bags. Robby and Samara stared at all the different-looking people. Not just those who looked "Italian" but Africans in native dress and Muslim women in long black chadors that covered their faces as well.

"Guess we're not the only tourists here," Chance quipped.

We dragged our bags outside. The air was cool, but the exhaust from the buses and cars smelled different from back home. Half a dozen men hurried toward us yelling *"Tassi! Tassi!"*

"Tassi?" Robby repeated.

"Taxi," Heavenly explained.

Most of the cars were smaller than in the States, and it was impossible to find a taxi large enough to fit all six of us. We finally squeezed into two small station wagons for the drive to Rome.

"Way cool!" Robby gasped as we entered a road filled with traffic. "Look at all the scooters and motorcycles!"

The traffic was crazy. Cars and scooters zipped past us at frightening speeds. Drivers waited at red lights only until other cars passed. Then they would go right through the red light even if it hadn't changed.

We finally got to Rome and found our hotel. Half the people we saw on the sidewalks were talking on cell phones as they walked.

"Look at that guy!" Robby pointed at a man on a scooter who was steering through the traffic with one hand while yelling into a cell phone.

Two men in green uniforms hurried out of the hotel and carried our bags into the lobby. Inside it wasn't nearly as large as the lobbies of American hotels, but the floors were marble and the walls were covered with old paintings.

"Ah, you are the Rands," said a handsome man in a dark suit standing behind the counter. "I am Sergio, the hotel manager. I know your parents well. They stay always here when they are in Rome."

Sergio gave us our room keys, and the men in the green uniforms took our bags upstairs.

"Anything you need, you call on me," Sergio said.

Heavenly yawned. *"Grazie, signore."*

We got our keys and went up to our rooms. Like the cars, the elevator was much smaller than in the States, and we had to split up. Upstairs, between my parents, Chance and Robby, Heavenly and Tyler, and Samara and me, we took up one whole floor of the hotel. The rooms were tiny. But they had beautiful window drapes, polished wooden furniture, and paintings on the walls.

"Oh, darn!" I heard Robby grumble from his room. "The TV's all in Italian."

"What did you expect?" Chance asked. "They'd be speaking Chinese?"

Samara yawned and rubbed her eyes. "I'm tired. Do you guys realize that right now it's four o'clock in the morning back home? Let's take a nap."

"No," Heavenly said. "Your Mom specifically said not to nap when we arrived."

"Why not?" asked Robby.

"Because she wants you to get used to Rome time," Heavenly explained. "If we stay up now and don't sleep until tonight, we'll get used to it faster."

"If we're not going to sleep, we should do the next best thing," said Robby.

"What's that?" Samara asked.

"Go eat," Robby said with a grin.

We took the elevator down to the lobby.

"All our money's American," said Chance. "We'd better exchange some into lira."

"You guys wait here and I'll go do it," said Heavenly.

"Wait a minute," I said. "How do you know how to exchange money? You've never been in a foreign country before."

Heavenly just smiled.

"I'll go with her," Chance said.

The rest of us waited in the hotel lobby while Chance followed Heavenly over to the cashier.

The elevator doors opened, and a boy about Chance's age came out with a girl around Samara's age. The girl's hair was light brown, and the boy's hair was dirty blond.

"You can bet they're not from Italy," Samara whispered.

"Probably from some Scandinavian country," I whispered back.

Oddly, as they passed us, we heard them speaking in what sounded like Italian. But while the language was different, the tone was universal. It was an annoyed older brother stuck baby-sitting his younger sister.

As they passed, the boy glanced in my direction. He had light blue eyes and when he saw me, the frown on his face became a little smile. Then he turned back to his sister and started grumbling again.

"I think he likes you," Samara whispered.

"How could he like me?" I asked back. "He doesn't even know me."

"Doesn't matter," Samara whispered back.

"Maybe not to *you*," I replied with a smirk.

Chance and Heavenly came back. Heavenly had a bunch of lira notes in her hand. I gave Chance a quizzical look.

"She knew *exactly* what to do," he said with a smirk. "Not only that, but she spoke in Italian."

"One good thing about being too scared to

sleep is I had a lot of time to study *The Idiot's Guide to Italian,*" she explained.

"I'm really thirsty," Robby said. "Can I have some money for a drink?"

Heavenly gave him a bill. Robby's eyes went wide.

"*Ten thousand* lira!" he cried. "Gee, thanks! I could probably buy a whole car for this!"

We watched as he hurried away to buy a lemonade. A moment later he was back with a little bottle and a big frown.

"I can't believe it!" he grumbled. "This cost six *thousand* lira!"

Chance pushed open the hotel door and held it so that Heavenly could wheel Tyler out in his stroller. But before Heavenly could go through the door, a familiar-looking blond woman stepped through, followed by a younger blond woman. They were both wearing hats and sunglasses, and carrying shopping bags. Suddenly I realized who the younger woman was.

"Jessica?" I said.

Chapter

16

Jessica stopped and tipped down her sunglasses. "Kit?"

"What in the world are you doing here?" I asked.

"We're staying here," Jessica said. "What are *you* doing here?"

"We're staying here, too," I said.

"What an amazing coincidence!" Jessica gasped, and glanced quickly at Chance.

It took a few moments for the initial shock to wear off. Then Jessica introduced her mom to us, and I introduced Heavenly and the members of my family. Mrs. Huffington asked where our parents were, and I explained about the meetings they had to attend.

"So where are you guys going?" Jessica asked, glancing at Chance again.

"We were just going out for some lunch," I said.

"So were we!" Jessica explained excitedly. "We just have to drop these things in our room. Why don't we all go together?"

Heavenly, Chance, and I shared a quick glance. I'm not sure lunch with Jessica was really what we had in mind for our first meal in Rome.

"What a great idea!" Samara gushed. "Let's do it. Then you can tell me everything about where to shop."

"Perfect," Jessica said. "Just give us a second and we'll be right down."

Jessica and her mom took the elevator upstairs. We waited in the hotel lobby.

"Can you believe they're staying at the same hotel as us?" Robby said. "What an amazing coincidence!"

"Amazing," I repeated.

Robby frowned. "You don't think it is?"

I rolled my eyes. The more I thought about it, the more I had serious doubts. Now I remembered telling Jessica that we'd be staying at a hotel near the Trevi Fountain where the British prime minister always stayed.

"I think we're really lucky," Samara said. "At least now I'll have someone to shop with, and I won't have to follow you around to those stupid ruins."

"You're right," said Robby. "And we won't have you around bugging us."

"That's enough from both of you," Heavenly said. "When you're in a faraway place and you meet someone you know, it's nice to have a drink with them."

"How would you know?" Robby asked. "I thought you'd never even been out of Soundview Manor."

"Heavenly's a quick study," I said and gave him a wink.

"Oh, right." Robby nodded. "Funny stuff, huh?"

"What are you guys talking about?" Samara asked.

"We'll tell you another time," I said.

It seemed as if a long time passed while we waited in the lobby.

"I thought they said they were going to be right down." Chance sounded a little annoyed.

"With Jessica, that's a relative term," I said.

"What does that mean?" Robby asked.

"Probably that she'll be right down . . . as soon as she showers, finds the right outfit, puts on fresh makeup, and does her hair," I said.

The words were hardly out of my mouth when the doors of the elevator opened and Jessica and her mom came out. As I expected, Jessica was wearing a different outfit.

Mrs. Huffington said she knew a nice little restaurant a few blocks away, and we all started to walk.

I noticed that Jessica positioned herself so that she was right in front of Chance, but before she could start a conversation with him, Samara popped up beside her.

"So tell me all about what you bought this morning," Samara said enviously.

The funny thing was, Jessica, who normally would have blown Samara off with a scathing look, decided to be friendly. Probably because she was trying to make a good impression on Chance.

"Well, you know how Italy is famous for its leather, so I got some fabulous shoes and a beautiful bag at Ferragamo," Jessica said.

"Didn't you just get here this morning?" I asked.

"Yes," Jessica replied. "Why?"

I couldn't believe it. It wasn't even lunchtime, and she'd already bought shoes and a bag!

Mrs. Huffington stopped under a bright yellow canopy. "Here we are."

The name of the restaurant was Il Costoso. A man in a dark suit opened the door for us. Inside the tables were covered with pink cloths, plates, and glasses. Around the tables stood more waiters than I'd ever seen in one restaurant before.

"Ah, Mrs. Huffington, good to see you again!" said the man in the dark suit. "You are in town for a few days of shopping?"

"Yes, Ernesto," Mrs. Huffington said. "And I have brought some friends, the Strands."

We all shared a slight grimace. Mrs. Huffington had already forgotten our last name!

Ernesto gestured for us to sit down at a table near the window. I happened to glance out the window and saw the blond-haired boy from the hotel and his sister passing on the sidewalk. They were *still* grumbling at each other!

I smiled. The blond-haired boy smiled back.

"Kit?" Robby said. "What do you want to drink?"

I turned and saw a waiter with a pad. "A Coke?"

"*Voglio Coca-Cola, per favore, signore,*" Jessica said.

"You know Italian?" Samara asked in awe.

"*Un poco,*" Jessica replied.

"I'm impressed," Chance said after Jessica finished ordering. "You sound almost fluent."

"Just in restaurants and stores," Jessica replied. "It's fine for my mom and me, since that's all we do when we're here."

"What about the museums and churches and ruins?" I asked. "I mean, all the history and art."

"We've done it," Jessica said. "I'm not saying it isn't interesting, but you have to spend so much time on your feet. It gets tiring after a while." She turned to Chance. "Besides, I like to save my energy for the *discoteca.*"

"*Discoteca?*" Samara repeated.

"That's what they call a dance club here," Jessica explained. "There's one on the top floor of our hotel."

Her comment hung in the air for a moment. It was obvious that she was hoping Chance would respond in some positive way, hopefully indicating that he'd love to go. But I knew Jessica was going to be disappointed. Chance wasn't the type who liked to go dancing.

"*Discoteca,* huh?" Chance said. "Sounds cool."

"Want to go tonight?" Jessica asked.

"Sure," said Chance.

I stared at my stepbrother in disbelief. I couldn't believe it! I just couldn't believe it!

Chapter 17

I have to admit that lunch was delicious. Everything—the bread, the pasta, the vegetables—tasted fresher than it did back home. After lunch Jessica and her mom wanted to go back to the hotel to hang out by the pool. But we wanted to walk around and see the city.

"I can't believe you agreed to go to dancing with her!" I said to Chance as we headed down the sidewalk.

"Why not?" Chance asked.

"Because you *hate* dancing," I said. "At least, you hate doing it in public."

"But I'm in Rome," Chance said. "It's perfect. I can go out dancing here, and no one will know me."

"I can't believe Jessica," I fumed. "I really can't!"

"What are you getting so bent out of shape about?" Chance asked.

"Are you for real?" I asked. "What do you think she's doing here?"

"Shopping and being on vacation," Chance said. "Sort of like us."

"But don't you wonder why, out of all the vacation spots in the world, she's here in Rome?" I asked. "And why she's staying at our hotel?"

"Our hotel?" Chance repeated with a sly grin. "I didn't know we owned it."

"You know what I mean," I said. "The only reason she's here and staying at our hotel is because of you."

"Right," Chance said with a smirk. "She and her mom came all the way to Italy just to see me."

"Yes!" I said. "I mean, they were probably planning a vacation anyway. Maybe they were even planning on coming to Rome. But believe me, Chance, it's no coincidence that they're in the same hotel as us."

"Well, it's a free world," Chance said.

"I know," I said with a sigh. "But I just can't believe the lengths she'll go to just to see you!"

Chance shrugged. Obviously, this didn't mean nearly as much to him as it did to me. "I don't see what the big deal is. But if you're so freaked out about us going dancing tonight, why don't you come, too?"

I stopped and stared at him. Why hadn't I thought of that?

"You know what?" I said with a smile. "That's exactly what I'm going to do!"

After sightseeing, we went back to our hotel to wash and rest before dinner. As usual when the family traveled, I was sharing a room with Samara.

After her shower, Samara came out of the bathroom wearing a white bathrobe and slippers supplied by the hotel.

"Can you believe Jessica?" she gushed. "I mean, knowing where to shop and how to speak Italian. She's so sophisticated!"

"Rich and spoiled is more like it," I grumbled.

My stepsister put her hand on her hip and shook her head. "If you were any greener, I'd need sunglasses."

I felt my jaw drop. "I am *not* jealous!"

"Totally," Samara said.

Before I could argue anymore, I heard knocking on my door. It was Robby. "Kit, Samara—Mom and Dad are here!"

Samara and I hurried out into the hall. A door was open and we went in. Mom and Dad, in their business clothes, were inside. Mom was holding Tyler in her arms and hugging him. Dad gave Samara a hug. Heavenly, Chance, and Robby were also there.

"How were your meetings?" Samara asked.

"Do you really think we're going to move here?" asked Robby.

"What about our house in Soundview Manor?" asked Chance.

"Wait until dinner," Mom said. "We'll answer all your questions then. But first we have some questions. How is everything back at home?"

Mom and Dad always wanted to know how we were doing in school and with our friends. We talked until dinnertime and then went back to our rooms to wash up. Samara put on a dress and nice shoes.

"What are you getting dressed up for?" I asked.

"Dinner," Samara answered.

"You really think everyone's going to be dressed up?" I asked.

"This is *Rome*, Kit," she replied. "Of course they're going to be dressed up."

A little while later we went to a beautiful outdoor restaurant where we sat at a table on the sidewalk under a big canvas umbrella.

Mom and Dad ordered big bottles of mineral water and soda. Cars and scooters zipped past on the street, and people passed on the sidewalk. A lot of them were talking into cell phones. Dad had Tyler on his knee, and he and Mom spent a lot of time playing with him.

"So what's the story, Mom?" I asked in between bites on delicious long, thin bread sticks.

"I'm talking to Telitalia about running their cellular phone division," Mom explained.

"What do you mean, talking?" Robby asked.

"Like I said before," Mom answered, "we have to decide if the job is right for me and if I'm right for the job."

"In other words, are they going to pay you enough?" Chance guessed.

"That's part of it," Mom answered.

"What about you, Dad?" I asked.

"I also have business here in Rome," Dad said. "And when I'm not in my own meetings, I'll be helping Mom negotiate her job."

Dinner began. I noticed that while the rest of us were eating pastas with delicious sauces, Mom and Dad were only drinking water and eating some bread sticks.

"No appetite?" I asked.

Mom and Dad exchanged an unhappy look.

"We have a dinner meeting later on," Mom explained.

"You have to go to a meeting *tonight?*" Robby asked, dismayed.

"I'm sorry, kids," Dad said. "We didn't realize how busy this week was going to be. Mom has to meet with dozens of people. We have a lot to do."

"Won't we get to see you at all?" Robby asked.

"We're going to try to be with you every spare moment we have," Mom said, then gave Tyler a kiss on his forehead.

After dinner Mom and Dad left for their meeting, and we walked back to the hotel.

"So who wants to go to the *discoteca?*" Samara asked as we entered the lobby.

"We'll all go up and check it out," Heavenly said, pushing Tyler in the stroller.

We took the elevator up to the top floor. The moment the elevator doors opened, we could hear music from the *discoteca* at the end of the hall.

"Wow, it's loud!" Samara gasped.

"Ear hurt!" Tyler yelped and put his little hands over his ears.

"I know, Tyler Tot," Heavenly said. "But we'll just be a minute."

She started to push the stroller down the carpeted hall.

"No!" Tyler cried, still clamping his hands over his ears. "Big loud."

Heavenly stopped and turned to Robby.

"Think you could take him back down to the lobby and wait for me there? I just want to make sure this is okay for Kit and Samara, and then I'll be right down and we'll go for some gelato."

Gelato is really creamy ice cream.

"Sure. For gelato I'll do anything." Robby took Tyler's stroller and started back toward the elevator.

Heavenly, Chance, Samara, and I continued down the hall. The _discoteca_ was lined with large darkened windows. The closer we got, the louder it got. Through the windows we could barely make out the multicolored flashing lights and the silhouettes of bodies dancing.

Chance opened the heavy, darkened glass door. Loud music and warm, perfumed air rushed out at us. Inside, part of the crowd was dancing. Other people were crammed into booths along the wall. Still others were standing near a refreshment stand.

The guys were all wearing long-sleeve shirts. Some were also wearing jackets. The girls were all wearing dresses. Samara shot me a look that said, "I told you so!"

We heard someone laugh. It was Jessica, in the middle of a crowd of admiring boys.

You could see that she was enjoying all the attention.

"Want to go over and say hello?" I asked Chance.

He shook his head.

"She invited you, remember?" I said.

"Looks like she's having a fine time without me," Chance said.

"But I thought you wanted to try it here in a foreign country," I said, half-teasing.

"I changed my mind," Chance said. "I'd rather go for gelato with Heavenly and the boys."

"I don't blame you," I said. "Me, too."

"Then Samara will have to come, too," Heavenly said. "I'm not leaving her here alone."

"That's not fair!" Samara whined. "I want to stay here."

"Don't bother to argue," Heavenly warned. "You're twelve years old, and you're not going to a *discoteca* by yourself. Period. End of discussion."

To my total surprise, Samara turned to me. "Kit, stay here just for a little while? *Please?* This is the only thing I came to Rome for!"

"You didn't come to Rome to go to a *discoteca*," I said. "You came to Rome because Mom wants to see if we'd be happy living here."

"But how will I know if I've never been to a *discoteca?*" she asked.

I was just about to tell her to take a major reality check when out of the crowd came the blond-haired boy from the hotel. He walked right up to me and smiled.

"Would you like to dance?" he asked.

Chapter

18

Talk about being caught by surprise. Out of the corner of my eye I glanced at my family. Samara was giving me a hopeful look, as if praying I'd say yes. Chance was sort of half-scowling, half-smiling. Heavenly was nodding, as if she approved.

"Uh, okay, sure," I said.

The blond boy reached for my hand. The next thing I knew, he was leading me to the dance floor.

"Just promise you'll keep an eye on Samara," Heavenly called behind me.

The weirdest thing has to be dancing with someone you don't know. I didn't even know his name! The other thing is, tall boys with long arms and legs don't tend to be great dancers. I mean, it's not their fault. It's just hard for them to know what to do with those long limbs.

And then there was the problem of keeping an eye on Samara, who was standing on the edge of the dance floor, looking around hopefully for someone who would pay attention to her.

"Kit?" Jessica caught me by surprise as she sidled up to me while dancing with no fewer than three handsome, dark-eyed Italian boys.

"Cute guy," she whispered in my ear as we danced.

"Yours, too," I said. "Or should I say, yours three."

"I know," she whispered back. "But where's Chance?"

"He was here before, but I think he changed his mind."

Jessica's jaw dropped, and she stopped dancing. "He was here and left?"

The next thing I knew, she turned away from the three boys she'd been dancing with.

One of the boys called after her in broken English. "Hey, pretty girl! Come back!"

But Jessica ignored him and left. The three boys frowned and began to grumble among themselves.

"Something is wrong?" asked the blond boy I was dancing with.

"Oh, uh, no," I quickly replied. "Sorry."

We started dancing again. Out of the corner of my eye I watched Samara, who was still looking hopefully at every boy who passed. Unfortunately, none of them looked back.

The song started to wind down and I started to get nervous. Now that the music was stopping, I might have to talk to the boy I was dancing with!

"Want something to drink?" he asked when we stopped dancing.

"Yes, but first, I want to know your name," I said.

"I am Rafael," he said.

"And I am Kit," I said.

"You are from Canada, yes?"

"No, I'm from the United States," I said.

Rafael frowned a little. "You are not sounding like you are from the United States."

"Well, I am," I said. "And you?"

"Como," he said. "Is in the north of Italy. Near Switzerland."

"I may not sound like I come from the United States, but you don't look like you're from Italy," I said.

Rafael nodded. "I know. But many Italians in the north have blond hair."

We both smiled, but neither of us seemed to know what to say. I started to get that nervous feeling again.

"So, uh, where's your sister?" I asked.

"She is with my parents," Rafael said.

"She doesn't like the *discoteca?*" I asked.

"She is not allowed," Rafael said. He nodded toward Samara, who was still standing by herself. "I see your sister is."

"Well, you know us wild Americans," I said with a nervous chuckle.

Rafael and I both got Cokes. By now another song had started. The music was loud.

Rafael leaned toward my ear. "Maybe we should go outside to the terrace. It is too loud to talk in here."

I have to admit that the idea of going outside sounded nice. Too bad. "I'm sorry, but I can't. I have to watch my sister."

Rafael nodded. "I understand."

But just then Samara came through the crowd toward us. The corners of her mouth were turned down.

"I want to go, Kit," she said. "No one's paying any attention to me. Will you take me back to the room?"

Now I had a problem. Samara wanted to go, but I wanted to stay. I glanced at Rafael and smiled weakly.

"We both can take her," he suggested.

Why not?

"Okay," I said.

A moment later Rafael, Samara, and I left the *discoteca* . . . just as Jessica came back, pulling Chance by the hand!

I stared at Chance in disbelief. Hadn't he just said a little while before that he'd changed his mind and wanted to go for gelato instead?

Jessica was grinning proudly as she led him past us. Chance gave me a sheepish grin as they passed us and went into the *discoteca*.

"Didn't Chance say he wanted to go with Heavenly?" Samara asked as we continued down the hall toward the elevator.

"Yes," I answered.

"Then how come he just went back into the *discoteca*?"

"Because what Jessica wants, Jessica gets."

"Gee." Samara sighed. "I wish I could be like that."

Heaven forbid, I thought. *One is enough!*

Rafael, Samara, and I got into the elevator and went back down to the room I was sharing with my stepsister. I opened the door and Samara went in and stopped. She looked back at me.

"I don't want to stay here alone, Kit," she said.

Oh, great . . . I thought. Now I couldn't go back to the disco with Rafael.

"Just lock the door," I said.

"It's scary," Samara complained.

"Samara, how many times have we gone away somewhere and stayed in a hotel and you didn't want to do what the rest of the family was doing so you stayed in your room?" I asked.

"But not at night," Samara said.

"It's okay," said Rafael. "You stay with your sister."

"Uh, could you just wait outside for a second?" I asked.

Rafael nodded. I went into the room, closed the door firmly, and turned to Samara.

"Why do I think you're only doing this because you know I want to be with Rafael?" I whispered.

Samara just shrugged. But I knew her. Misery loved company, and if Samara wasn't having fun, then she was going to make sure no one was having fun.

"I'm going back to the *discoteca*," I said.

"I'll tell Mom," Samara threatened.

I could have killed her. "Okay, suppose I invite Rafael to come in here and watch TV or something?"

My stepsister made her eyes go wide in mock horror. "You can't invite a boy into our room! Mom would have a fit."

"Only because you'd just have to tell her, wouldn't you?" I said.

"Mom would be very disappointed in me if I didn't," Samara replied with a sniff.

It was hopeless. My stepsister was determined to make sure I wouldn't be with Rafael. I'd been through this so many times before with her that it didn't even make me mad anymore. This was just the way it was.

"Well, the one thing you're not going to stop me from doing is saying good night to him," I said, and went back out into the hall, closing the door behind me.

Rafael was waiting.

"I'm sorry, but I have to stay with her," I explained.

"Don't be sorry," he said. "I understand."

We smiled at each other for a moment.

"So, uh, tomorrow maybe," he said.

"Tomorrow we're supposed to visit the Coliseum," I said.

"Me, too!" Rafael brightened for a moment, then stopped smiling. "With my parents and sister."

"Still, maybe we'll see each other," I said.

"Yes, that would be nice."

We smiled at each other again. There didn't seem to be anything more to say, but I didn't want the evening to end. Suddenly I stretched up on my tiptoes and kissed him on the cheek.

Rafael looked surprised, then gave me a big

grin. "Tomorrow, then." He turned and went back down the hall.

Feeling giddy and warm all over, I went into my room. I couldn't believe what I'd just done. Then again, like Chance said, we were in a foreign country where no one knew us. So what the heck!

Chapter

19

$\mathbf{S}$amara and I watched the Italian version of MTV for a while. The funny thing was that most of the videos were in English anyway. We'd just gotten into bed and turned off the lights when someone knocked on the door.

"Who is it?" I called.

"Heavenly. Could you open up?"

I went to the door and opened it. Heavenly was standing in the hall and her brow was wrinkled. She looked worried.

"Have you seen Chance?" she asked.

"He and Jessica went to the *discoteca*," I said.

Heavenly blinked with surprise. "Chance went back to the disco?"

"Jessica wanted him to," I said. "She doesn't take no for an answer."

Heavenly glanced at her watch. "It's almost one in the morning."

The words were hardly out of her mouth when the elevator doors at the end of the hall opened and Jessica, Chance, and Sergio, the hotel manager, came out. Chance's shirt was torn and smeared with blood. He had a big bruise under his right eye, and his hair was wild.

Meanwhile, Jessica was doing her best Florence Nightingale routine. Sergio had a frown on his face.

"Chance, what happened to you?" Heavenly asked, going to him.

"Nothing," Chance replied with his typical shrug. "We just ran into a little problem."

"*Signorina,*" Sergio said. "You are his sister?"

"No, but he is my responsibility," Heavenly replied.

"I'm sorry, I do not understand this word," Sergio said.

"*Responsabilità,*" Heavenly said.

The next thing I knew, the two of them launched into a heated conversation in Italian. Knowing Heavenly, neither Chance nor I was particularly surprised, but Jessica looked as if she'd just seen a talking horse.

"She knows Italian?" Jessica asked, pulling me aside.

Todd Strasser

"Looks like it," I replied. Heavenly and Sergio were speaking so fast, I wasn't sure I would have understood them even if they'd been speaking in English!

"So what happened in the *discoteca?*" I asked.

"Those Italian boys." Jessica shook her head wearily. "You dance with them a little, flirt a little, and the next thing you know, they think they own you."

"You left them and then came back with Chance?" I said.

"Right." Jessica nodded. "They didn't like that at all. But Chance was so brave. When they started getting mean, he immediately defended my honor."

"Looks like it hurt him more than it hurt you," I observed.

"You should see those three boys," Jessica said with a wink. "I think they got the worst of it."

Finally Heavenly and Sergio appeared to reach an understanding. Sergio marched away toward the elevator. Heavenly turned to Chance and crossed her arms.

"Next time you get into a fight, try not to pick it in the hotel," she said.

"Hey, I didn't pick it," Chance replied. "Those guys did."

"Well, it doesn't matter now," said Heavenly.

"You're banned from the *discoteca* for the rest of the trip."

"Fine, I didn't like that scene anyway," Chance said.

"You didn't?" Jessica slid her arm through Chance's and looked very disappointed.

"Well, I mean, it was okay, but nothing great," Chance said. "We can always go somewhere else."

Now Jessica smiled. "Good." She gave him a gooey, dreamy look.

I wanted to barf.

"Isn't your mother wondering where you are?" Heavenly asked her.

"Oh, she's probably fast asleep," Jessica said.

"Well, I think it's time for Chance and Kit to get to bed," Heavenly said. "So, we'll see you tomorrow."

Jessica turned to Chance, stretched up on her toes, and gave him a quick peck on the cheek. "*A domani.*"

She went off down the hall, walking as if her feet weren't quite touching the ground.

"Well, guys"—Chance yawned—"nothing like a good fight before you go to bed. See you in the morning."

He went to the room he shared with Robby. I peeked inside. Robby was in bed, wrapped in a blanket, fast asleep. Chance went in.

As soon as the door closed, I turned to Heavenly.

"She kissed him," I groaned.

"I know." Heavenly didn't look happy.

"I mean, you know I've always wanted Chance to have a girlfriend," I said.

"You just never imagined it would be Jessica Huffington," Heavenly added.

"Not in a million years," I admitted.

"But you have to admit that it makes sense," Heavenly said.

"Sense?" I repeated. "How?"

"Chance is the most desirable boy in the school," Heavenly said.

"Right," I said. "And Jessica wants only the best. But I really don't see them together. I mean, they're so different."

"You've never heard of opposites attracting?" Heavenly asked.

"Not those two opposites," I prayed. *"Please!* Not those two!"

Chapter
20

The next morning Mom and Dad got us up really early just to spend some time with us before they hurried off to their meetings.

They really freaked when they saw Chance's face, but Chance did a good job of making it sound as if it was a one-in-a-million kind of thing and would never happen again.

After Mom and Dad left, we kids and Heavenly gathered on the hotel veranda to eat breakfast. The veranda was on the roof. It was a beautiful terrace with large brick-colored tiles on the floor, and tables covered with cream-colored tablecloths. Red and yellow flowers and leafy green vines grew over the railing. Pastries, yogurt, cereal, and pitchers of juice were set out on a long table on one side of the veranda.

Bleary-eyed and tired, we slumped down at

the table set with plates and glasses. A single flower stood in the thin glass vase in the middle of the table. The warm Roman sun shone down on us, but I had a feeling the beauty surrounding us went unnoticed. Samara, Chance, and I slouched in our chairs.

"You sure are a lively bunch this morning," Heavenly said with a smirk.

"We should have gone back to sleep," I replied with a yawn. "Don't you know it's the middle of the night back in the States?"

"We're not back in the States," Heavenly said. "We're here and it's nine in the morning. Besides, if you look around you might notice that except for us, the veranda is empty. If I'd waited any longer, we'd be too late for breakfast."

"So?" I groaned. "Why couldn't we skip breakfast and sleep until lunch?"

"Because we're in Rome and there's lots to see," Heavenly said. "You guys can catch up on your sleep when you get home."

"Oh, wow! Muffins!" Robby, the only one of us who seemed to have any energy, crossed the veranda and returned with a plate heaped with rolls. "Croissants with powdered sugar on the outside and the jelly already inside! Cool!"

"They're called coronets," Heavenly informed him.

"Hhhmmmmmm, these are good!" Crumbs fell from his chin and fingers.

"Is there any orange juice in Italy?" A muffled groan came from the opposite end of the table. It was Chance. His head was buried in his arms and his hair was wild in knots.

"It's called *il sugo d'arancia*," Heavenly said.

"Call it whatever you want," Chance replied without expression. He lifted his head. The bruise under his eye had turned darker, and the left side of his mouth was swollen. "Can I have some?"

"*Sì, Signore*, it's right over there." Heavenly pointed at the table across the veranda. A large, round glass pitcher of orange juice was sitting on it.

"Oh, man," Chance groaned. "I'm so wiped out. Can't someone get it for me? Come on, Robby, you're full of energy. How about it?"

But Robby's cheeks were bulging with food. He shook his head. "Sorry, partner, but I'm in full sitting and eating mode."

Chance turned and gave me a pleading look, but I was so tired I felt cemented to my chair. Samara wasn't even awake anymore. She'd put her head down on her arms and was lightly snoring. Chance turned to Heavenly.

"Can't you do some magic or something?" he

asked. "We all know you can do it. And I've been up all night fighting."

Heavenly gave us an uncertain look.

"He's right, Heavenly," Robby said with bulging cheeks. "I mean, after that thing with the first-class tickets, who do you think you're fooling?"

Heavenly sighed. "Can I trust you?"

The three of us nodded eagerly. Heavenly glanced at Samara, who was still snoring away.

"I'm not sure I can trust her," she said.

"You're smart," I said.

"So what about the sucoranga or whatever you called it?" Chance reminded her.

Heavenly rolled her eyes. "You are too much, *signore.*"

She reached up to her left ear. From out of nowhere a red ladybug started to crawl up the stem of the flower in the vase. Across the room the pitcher of orange juice began to float in the air.

"This is mad cool," Robby gasped.

"Hush!" I whispered and nodded in Samara's direction. "Heavenly doesn't want her to know, remember?"

Meanwhile, Heavenly nodded in Chance's direction and the juice floated over to his glass. We watched as the pitcher poured itself into

Chance's glass and then started to float back across the room.

"Hey, wait a minute!" I said. "What about the rest of us?"

As if it had a mind of its own, the pitcher stopped in midair and returned to our table, where it poured orange juice into the rest of our glasses. Then it headed back toward the long table where it placed itself back down.

"Thanks," Chance mumbled.

"Yeah, thanks," echoed Samara, who raised her head just enough to open her mouth and sip some orange juice. Knowing that she had no idea what Heavenly had just done, the rest of us shared a smile. But Samara was too tired to notice.

Robby took a sip of the orange juice and grimaced. "Ech! They've got it here, too."

Chance frowned and took a sip. The frown turned into a smile. "Oh, cool! *Real* orange juice!"

Robby gave Heavenly a puzzled look. "Are you Italian or something?"

Heavenly smiled. "Just because they serve fresh orange juice here and I serve it at home doesn't make me Italian."

Robby took another sip. "Hmmm. I think they did it on purpose to make us think it's the same here as at home."

"They'd have to do a lot more than just make the orange juice the same," I said, thinking of Rafael. Suddenly the idea of staying in Rome didn't sound so bad.

Everyone was quiet for a moment. Samara put her head back down on her arms and started to snore again.

"*There* you are!" a voice behind us suddenly said. We all looked around. Jessica was coming toward us.

"*Buon giorno!*" She came up behind Chance and wrapped her arms around his neck. "My hero!"

"Oh, hey, Jessica," Chance replied sleepily.

"Huh?" Samara's eyes lifted from closed to half-mast.

Jessica pulled up a chair from a neighboring table and squeezed it in between Samara and Chance.

Screech! The chair sliding along the tiled floor was like nails on a chalkboard to our ears, and we all winced.

"Oops!" Jessica pressed her fingers against her lips. "Sorry!"

I couldn't imagine where she got all that energy from, unless it was the sheer excitement of being close to Chance.

"So, how is everyone this morning?" she asked without taking her eyes off Chance.

"Great!" Robby answered, using the back of his hand to wipe the powdered sugar from his lips.

"Use this," Heavenly said, handing him a cloth napkin.

"And what are *we* doing today?" Jessica asked.

Out of the corner of my eye I caught the look Heavenly gave me.

"Aren't you going shopping?" I asked.

"Not today," Jessica answered. "Mom's going to the beauty spa. I told her I'd hang out with you guys."

Another day with Jessica, I thought. *What fun!*

"We're going to check out the Coliseum—right, kids?" Heavenly asked.

"Do they have gelato there?" Robby asked.

"If not there, then nearby," Heavenly replied.

"Then let's go!" Robby said eagerly.

"Weren't you the one who said you were going to hate Italy?" Chance asked.

"That was before I tasted the food," Robby replied.

"The next thing he'll have to try is the broccoli," I joked.

"I had some last night that was fabulous," Jessica said. "With olive oil, garlic, and lemon juice."

"Really? It actually sounds like it might be good!" Robby said.

"Amazing," Heavenly said, shaking her head.

A little while later we gathered in the lobby. Heavenly, Chance, Robby, and I were dressed for trekking in T-shirts and jeans. Samara, of course, was wearing a dress and dress shoes.

"Do you think there are any clothes stores around the Coliseum?" she asked. "So I could shop while you sightsee?"

"Maybe the Huffingtons would like to adopt you," I said. "You're much more like them than like us."

Samara stuck her tongue out at me. I have to admit that half the reason I said that was to see how Chance would react. But either he was too tired to react or he just didn't care.

The elevator doors opened, and Jessica came out wearing clunky high-heeled shoes and a miniskirt that was so tight around her thighs that it shortened her strides to about five inches. She had a pair of sunglasses stuck on top of her head like a crown.

"Ready to go to the Coliseum?" Heavenly asked.

"Are you sure you don't want to go to Via del Corso instead?" Jessica asked.

"Why would we want to go there?" Robby asked.

"They have great shops," Jessica said.

"Wouldn't you like to see the Coliseum?" Chance asked.

There was a slight suggestion of a frown on Jessica's forehead, but it quickly disappeared as she bit her lip and exclaimed, "Oh, sure! The Coliseum is my favorite!"

We left the hotel and walked down the sidewalk.

"The Coliseum's got to be totally cool." Robby's attention switched to Jessica. "With the gladiators, and the fights between the slaves and the wild animals. What do you like best about it?"

"Well, uh . . ." Jessica stumbled on her words. It was obvious that she was trying to think of something to say. "I guess the shows and concerts and stuff."

"Concerts?" I repeated with a scowl.

"Yeah, I mean, it's a coliseum, right?" Jessica said. "Don't they have concerts there?"

Robby looked puzzled. "Not in the past thousand years. It's nothing but ruins now."

"Oh, right, I knew that." Jessica had a big grin on her face. The rest of us shared uncertain glances.

"All right, troops!" Heavenly spoke up. "Let's get going! The Coliseum opens soon, and it's been waiting fifteen hundred years just for us."

We headed out into the busy streets. Our hotel wasn't all that far from the Coliseum but walking was a problem. Most of the cars were half the size of the cars in America, and the drivers seemed to like squeezing past each other and past us.

"Jerk!" Jessica yelled at one car that zipped past with only inches to spare. She used that as an excuse to slip her arm through Chance's.

"I'd like to have a Chevy Suburban in this traffic." Chance, who was finally waking up, chuckled. Jessica gripped his arm as if her life depended on it. Mostly, I thought, because she had to take so many little steps for every one Chance made.

"Are we almost there?" Robby asked.

"Almost," Heavenly replied. "Ah, there we are."

Ahead sat the Coliseum. Some of the walls had tumbled down with the ages, and its crumbling stone arcs were a drab gray. Still, you couldn't help admiring it, and the fact that it was nearly two thousand years old. Heavenly bought us tickets, and we went inside.

"This place is amazing!" Robby said as we gazed down at the maze of stone passageways that were all that remained of the floor. "I mean, just think of how big it was when all its walls were still standing."

"Is there a gift shop?" Samara asked.

We walked around the first level and then up to the next. I found it easy to imagine the place filled with Romans cheering and shouting as men fought for their lives against other men or animals.

"Not all the gladiators were slaves," Heavenly said. "Some were paid professional fighters."

"What a way to make a living," Robby said in awe.

"I could see you doing it," Jessica said to Chance. "Like the way you took on those three boys last night. You were fearless."

"Yeah, Chance," Robby said with a laugh. "How about taking on a few gladiators next? Or maybe some lions and hippos."

"Kit?" someone said.

I turned around and found Rafael coming toward me. He was followed by the rest of his family.

"You are here, just like you said." Rafael smiled. I could tell he was glad to see me. I was glad to see him, too.

Rafael introduced me to his parents. They were both tall. His mother had reddish hair. His father's hair was sandy blond. His sister's name was Maria.

Next, it was my turn to introduce my family. That was always a bit of a chore.

"This is Heavenly, Chance, Robby, Samara, Tyler"—I had to pause to take a breath—"and Jessica."

Rafael's father nodded sternly. "A big family for America, yes?"

"Well, not exactly," I began to explain. "You see, Jessica's a friend, Heavenly's the nanny, and the rest of us are actually stepbrothers and stepsisters."

Rafael's father frowned, but his mother nodded as if she understood. "Like the Brady Bunch?"

"Well, uh, sort of." I forced a smile on my face.

Maria tugged at her father's hand and spoke in very whiny Italian. I kind of got the feeling she wanted to go.

Rafael's mom said something in Italian to Rafael, who frowned and spoke back in a voice that seemed to disagree. I noticed that Rafael was carrying a small artist's sketch pad, and he kept gesturing to it.

The discussion went back and forth a few times, then Rafael turned to me.

"Maria isn't liking this," he explained. "My parents will take her away. But I am wanting to stay and draw."

"Oh, uh, you're welcome to come with us," I said. "I think we're going to the Roman Forum next."

Rafael turned to his parents again. Another conversation in Italian ensued. I couldn't understand a word they said, but it was pretty obvious that Rafael was trying to convince his parents to let him go with us. Neither his mom nor his dad looked very happy about it.

Finally Rafael kissed his mother on both cheeks. *"Ciao, Mamma."*

"Ciao, Rafael," said his mother. *"A più tardi."*

His parents started away with Maria.

Rafael turned to me. "Okay, I go with you."

We left the Coliseum and headed toward the Roman Forum. As we started through the ruins with a few tall columns here and there, Heavenly explained that these were really the remains of a collection of many forums and temples. She talked about the different emperors who ruled Rome during those times. I hate to admit that I wasn't paying much attention. Most of my thoughts concerned Rafael.

Rafael and I fell behind the others.

"You sure it's okay with your parents?" I asked him.

"When I go with my parents, we do . . . how do you say? All together all the time?"

"You do everything together?" I said.

"Sì! We do everything. We do too much together!"

"Boy, can I relate to that," I said.

Rafael frowned. "Relate? I do not understand."

"It means I know exactly how you feel," I said.

Rafael smiled. He had a great smile. Even though we couldn't communicate very well, I felt a big warm feeling toward him.

We strolled among the ruins, falling farther and farther behind Heavenly and the others. At one point Chance glanced back at us.

"Is hurt your brother's face?" Rafael asked.

"He got into a fight last night," I explained.

Rafael frowned, then balled his hands into fists and pretended he was fighting. "Like this?"

"Yes," I said. "He's sort of a magnet for that kind of thing."

"Magnet?" Rafael repeated, puzzled.

"It means he attracts the wrong kind of people," I tried to explain.

Rafael was still frowning. "Attracts? If I attracts you, this means we fight?"

"I hope not!" I said with a laugh.

Rafael asked if we could stop so that he could sketch the top of a column. While Heavenly and the others kept strolling, I sat and watched over his shoulder as he drew. I couldn't believe how fast and well he could sketch.

"You're like a professional!" I said.

"That is good, I hope," Rafael said with a small grin.

"Yes, very good," I said.

"Thank you."

I could have sat and watched him draw all day, but after a while it was time for lunch. Heavenly led us to a street corner where we waited while cars, scooters, and motorcycles raced past.

Suddenly a pack of motorcycles roared by. The drivers were all wearing tight, brightly colored outfits. Their motorcycles were just as shiny and brightly colored as their clothes. As they passed, one of them glanced at us and suddenly slowed down.

At first I didn't recognize him, but that was probably because one of his eyes was black and blue and nearly swollen shut. Then I realized he was one of the boys from the *discoteca* the night before. He stared at Chance, then gunned his motorcycle with a roar and raced after his friends.

"He knows you?" Rafael asked.

"From the *discoteca* last night," I explained.

There was a break in the traffic.

"Let's go, everyone," Heavenly said.

We crossed the street and started along the sidewalk. Suddenly the group of guys on the motorcycles roared around the corner and stopped on the street beside us.

I counted five motorcycles. Two of them carried drivers and passengers. That made seven guys altogether.

"*Teppesti*," Rafael mumbled.

"What?" I whispered.

"Is like a gang," he whispered. "Very bad."

Chapter

21

We watched silently as they lined their motorcycles along the sidewalk, facing the curb like a row of horses in the Old West. All together they slowly got off.

"Just like the bad guys in the movies!" Robby whispered.

"Yeah." Chance smirked. "These dudes have been watching too many spaghetti westerns."

I recognized the other two boys from the night before. One had a big red lump on his forehead, and the other had a swollen, split lip.

"Chance, I'm getting worried," I whispered under my breath.

"Don't sweat it," Chance said. "I handled these guys last night."

"Last night there were only three," I pointed out. "Now it's seven against one."

"Seven against two," Rafael said, stepping beside my stepbrother.

"Hey, you!" one of the boys grunted.

"Say what?" Chance answered.

"You are that pest!" another grumbled.

"But I'm the best pest / the pest with zest / a better pest than the rest," Chance answered, as if he was rapping.

The *teppesti* frowned and scowled at each other. It was obvious that they didn't understand Chance's rap.

Suddenly the gang came forward.

"You! I punch you!" One threw a punch at Chance. My stepbrother dodged it and backed away. Jessica screamed. Rafael and Chance raised their fists and faced the seven *teppesti*. I didn't care how good Chance and Rafael were at fighting, the odds were still against them.

I spun around and looked at Heavenly. She was busy backing Tyler's stroller away so that he wouldn't get caught in the fray.

I caught her eye and tugged at my left ear. Heavenly got the message and reached up to her left ear. A second later I heard a creaking sound. One of the motorcycles started to lean toward the others.

Crash! It fell into the motorcycle next to it. *Crash! Crash! Crash! Crash!*

Like a row of dominoes, each motorcycle fell into the next, knocking it over.

The gang of *teppesti* forgot about Chance and Rafael and hurried to their motorcycles, which now lay in a pile in the street. They stood over the fallen cycles with sad, upset expressions on their faces. Like little boys who'd just broken their favorite toys.

"*Mamma mia!*" one wailed.

"*Mio Dio!*" yelled another.

One of them tried to pull his motorcycle back up, but as he did, it left a big scratch on the motorcycle under it.

"*Idiota!*" yelled one of the *teppesti* at the guy who'd tried to pick up his motorcycle.

"*Ficcatelo tra i denti!*" the guy yelled back.

The first guy took a swing at the second.

The second one swung back.

Somehow he missed the first one, but managed to hit a third one in the back. The third one spun around and swung at the second one, but somehow hit a fourth instead.

I couldn't believe what bad aim those guys had . . . until I turned and saw that Heavenly was tugging at her left ear again. She was rigging the fight!

Pretty soon the whole gang was fighting with one another! In the distance we could hear funny wailing sirens, and I caught sight of some flashing blue lights. Like the ones the *polizia* had on their cars and motorcycles.

"I think this might be a very good time for us to continue our tour," Heavenly suggested with a soft chuckle.

We started up the sidewalk just as the *polizia* arrived in their little blue-and-white police cars.

Once again, Jessica attached herself to Chance's arm. "That was so brave!" she said. "I can't believe you were ready to take on all seven of them by yourself!"

"Seven against one doesn't sound like fun," Chance replied. "But you have to wait until the fight's begun / The last man standing is the man who's won / It's the dirty deed when the deed is done."

Following behind the others, Rafael scowled at me. "Your stepbrother is rapping good. But I am not sure I understand."

"Don't worry about it," I said. "I'm not sure any of us understands him, either."

Rafael smiled at me and I smiled back. A warm tingly feeling raced through me. But the moment was broken when Robby said, "Hey, what do you say we get some pizzas for lunch?"

Suddenly I knew that what I really wanted wasn't pizza, but some time alone with Rafael. But how?

Chapter

22

We found a pizzeria and took a table on the sidewalk. It may have been only our second day in Italy, but Robby was already fluent when it came to ordering a pizza and a Coke.

"Una margherita e una Coke, per favore," he said to the waiter.

Everyone else put in their orders, and then Heavenly turned to me. "And what would you like, Kit?"

"A little time alone with Rafael," I whispered. The rest of my family was busy watching the people on the sidewalk stroll past.

Heavenly frowned for a split second, then caught on and smiled. "When?"

"How about after lunch?" I asked. "Just to walk around and talk without being bothered."

Heavenly nodded. I knew she understood. That wasn't the problem.

"You know your parents expect me to keep an eye on you," she said.

"I know," I said, "but this is important."

"Well, all right. Just promise me you'll be back at the hotel by dinnertime?"

"Triple promise."

"Okay," Heavenly said. "Make it look like you two snuck off when nobody else was looking. Rome's a big, busy city. It definitely wouldn't make sense for us to try to go find you."

I grinned. "You're the best, Heavenly."

A little while later, after lunch, Rafael and I "disappeared" down a narrow alley.

We spent the rest of the afternoon walking and talking. We sat on the Spanish steps and Rafael sketched while I watched pigeons give themselves baths in the fountain. We went to the Trevi Fountain and threw coins over our left shoulders and into the water to make sure we'd return to Rome someday. We sat on a bench and slurped frozen lemon *granitas* through straws.

Mostly we talked—about school and friends and parents and annoying younger sisters. It seemed amazing that we had so much to talk about. Rafael was funny and charming. Even though we came from different countries, I felt as if we had a lot in common.

Later when we got back to the hotel, both Chance and Samara gave me looks. Chance's was a smile, as if he was happy for me. Samara's was more of a leer. Neither of them said a word, however, and I had to believe it was because Heavenly warned them not to.

Rafael and I spent the next day together with my family. Mom and Dad took the afternoon off and joined us for a tour of the Vatican and St. Peter's, and then they took us all to dinner.

The next night they had another dinner meeting, so Heavenly gave me permission to have dinner with Rafael's family. Rafael's parents were kind of strict and hardly ever smiled. I got the feeling that they weren't particularly happy about their son having an American girl around.

If we weren't with my family or his, we just stayed by ourselves in the hotel lobby. In fact, we spent so much time sitting in the lobby that the concierges got to know us by name. To be honest, it hardly mattered to me where we were. Just about the only thing that really mattered to me was being with Rafael.

One evening Robby found a place that showed movies in English. He, Chance, Jessica, Samara, and my parents decided to go, but they'd be out too late for Tyler. I'd already seen the movie back in Soundview, so they left

Heavenly, Tyler, and me to go for dinner alone.

We found a cute sidewalk restaurant and ordered Cokes and pasta. We'd had a big lunch with my parents that day and Heavenly wasn't really hungry. Tyler and I decided to share a bowl of pasta. Tyler preferred his pasta plain and with butter.

"Susgetti," said Tyler, who couldn't pronounce *spaghetti*.

"Here they call it pasta," Heavenly said.

"Basta," Tyler said.

"I think he's better off saying susgetti," I said.

Heavenly and I shared a laugh. I realized that this was the first time we'd been together without the others since the flight over.

"Maybe you could tell me more about you know what," I said as we ate.

"What would you like to know?" she asked.

"Well, why do you think you can do it?" I asked.

"I don't know," Heavenly said.

"It's so weird," I said.

"Think of how weird it is for me," she said. "I mean, being able to do these things and having no idea why or what to do with them. I was lucky I had Cocci."

"Why?" I asked.

"Because she taught me," Heavenly said, "only to use it for good things."

"What about fun things?" I asked.

"Only if it's harmless fun," Heavenly said.

We talked a little more, but after a while I ran out of questions. It may seem strange, but once you get used to someone having special powers, so what? It's like, back to normal life.

"Just one other thing," I said.

Heavenly looked a little surprised.

"No, it's not about special powers," I said. "It's about a special guy."

"Rafael?"

"No, your special guy. Wes."

Heavenly blinked. "Oh."

"I noticed that things seemed different between you two in the van," I said.

"Really?"

"Don't play dumb, Heavenly. Something's changed between you two."

Heavenly sighed. "Okay, if you really must know the truth, we've been seeing each other."

I couldn't believe it! "When? How? How come I didn't know?"

"We see each other on the weekends," Heavenly said.

I stared at her in disbelief. "Is it serious?"

Heavenly shrugged but smiled in a way to indicate that it was.

I threw my arms around her neck and gave her a hug. "I'm so happy for you!"

"I assume you're going to see Rafael tonight?" she said once I let go.

I nodded. "He's having dinner with his parents. He said he'd find me afterward." I gazed around for a moment. "This reminds me of that scene in *Lady and the Tramp*. You know, the one where they're having dinner outside?"

"Oh, yes," Heavenly said with a grin. "That was always one of my favorite movies."

"Me, too." I sighed wistfully and wished Rafael was there. Meanwhile, I lifted a forkful of pasta to my lips and ate it. One strand was longer than the others, and I sort of sucked it in.

But it seemed like it would never end. I looked over and saw that the other end went all the way to Tyler!

Heavenly had a big grin on her face. A ladybug landed on the edge of the pasta bowl.

"Just like the movie!" I cried. "You did this on purpose!"

"Just a little harmless fun," Heavenly said with a wink.

Suddenly I heard a motor scooter ride up on the sidewalk. There was nothing unusual about that. The Italians did it all the time.

"I hope I am not an interruption," someone said.

I spun around in my seat. It was Rafael, on a blue scooter!

"Where'd you get that?" I asked.

"I am renting it," he said, getting off. "May I join you?"

"Your timing couldn't be better," Heavenly said, getting up. "I was just about to put Tyler to bed. Why don't you keep Kit company?"

Rafael took a seat, and Heavenly gave me a wink and left. She was the best. Just the best!

Chapter

23

The next evening I was in my room with Samara after a day of sightseeing. I took a shower and came out of the bathroom, thinking about Rafael. Samara was lying on her stomach on her bed, watching Italian MTV.

"Would you please stop humming?" she grumbled.

"Huh?" She caught me by surprise. "I didn't realize I was humming."

"Oh, please," my stepsister groaned. "You've been humming for *days*. Ever since you fell in love with Rafael."

"I haven't fallen in love with anyone," I said.

"Yeah, right." Samara rolled her eyes in disbelief.

"Well, I admit I like him," I said.

"Hooray for you," Samara grumbled sourly.

"Some sisters might actually be happy for me," I said.

Just then there was a knock on our door, and Mom came in. She was wearing her business clothes and had dark rings under her eyes. It was obvious that she hadn't gotten much sleep lately.

"Hey, kids." She held out her arms, and we each gave her a hug. "Have a good day?"

"Yes," I said.

"No," said Samara.

"Why not?" Mom asked.

"I don't like it here, Mom," my stepsister said. "I hope we don't move here."

"Let's talk about it at dinner in half an hour, okay?" Mom said.

"Can Rafael come?" I asked. The question had become second nature to me. We'd had practically every meal together since we'd met.

"He's a very charming young man, and on any other night I'd say of course," Mom said. "But not tonight. We've got important family matters to discuss. If it's any consolation, Jessica won't be there, either."

Mom left and Samara and I looked at each other.

"Sounds serious," Samara said.

"Think tonight's the night we decide?" I asked, thinking mostly of Rafael.

"I hope so, as long as it's deciding to go home," Samara muttered.

The funny thing was, I couldn't think of anything I wanted less.

Chapter

24

That night we went to a funny restaurant called the Grotto Azure. The walls were covered with rough cement like the inside of a cave, and there were big paintings of Naples after Mt. Vesuvius erupted. A small band played songs, and a man in a tuxedo sang in a loud booming voice like an opera singer.

We sat at a round table with a high chair for Tyler. Tonight Mom and Dad ordered a big meal and even had a glass of wine. We got all the way to coffee and dessert, and Mom and Dad still hadn't said anything. But then Dad cleared his throat and gave Mom a meaningful nod. I braced myself. Mom took a sip of her coffee and pressed her fingertips together.

"Well, you're probably wondering why we called this meeting," she said with a chuckle.

Everyone laughed nervously.

"It's because the time has come for us to decide whether or not we move here," she said.

The rest of us around the table gave one another uncomfortable looks.

"What about your job?" I asked.

"The job is good, but not great," Mom answered. "Certainly not great enough to insist that our entire family move here. That's why we want to hear what each of you thinks. Dad and I have agreed that everyone in the family has to decide whether we should move here or not."

Once again we all looked at one another.

"Including Tyler?" Robby asked.

"No, he's a bit too young," Dad said with a laugh. "Mom and I thought we'd start with the oldest and work our way down. So we'll start with Chance."

My stepbrother sat up straight in his seat. "You're asking *me* whether I think we should move here or not?"

Mom and Dad nodded.

"Well . . ." Chance scratched his head. "I guess I have to say that I'd rather not. I mean, it's interesting here and everything, but I'd just as soon go back home."

Dad turned to me. "Kit?"

"I want to stay." The words were out of my mouth before I realized it.

"Of course she does," Samara grumbled and made a face. "She's in love."

Mom smiled sweetly. "Rafael's a very nice young man."

"I'm not in love with him," I said, feeling my face start to burn with a blush.

"Then why do you want to stay so badly?" Samara asked.

"I . . ." The truth was, I didn't know what to say. My stepsister was basically right. All I could think about was being with Rafael.

"I think we can move on to the next person," Dad said. "So, Samara, has Rome lived up to your fashion expectations?"

"I can't wait to get out of here," Samara growled.

"I take it that's a no," Dad said, and turned to Robby. "As I recall, you were the one who hated the idea the most, Robby. Still feel that way?"

"Dad, have you tasted the gelato?" Robby asked.

"Yes."

"The pizza?"

"Yes."

"The French fries?"

"Well, no," Dad said.

"That explains it," Robby said.

"Explains what?" Mom asked.

"If Dad had tried all three of those things, he'd know that I'm ready to live here for the rest of my life," Robby said.

"You're serious?" Mom asked.

"Mom, I've even eaten the *broccoli*," Robby said.

"He's serious," Heavenly assured them.

Dad turned to Mom. "Well, it's a tie. Two for and two against."

"I was afraid this would happen," Mom said.

"Shouldn't Heavenly have a vote?" Robby asked.

Mom blinked. Dad looked as if he didn't know what to say.

"No, I shouldn't," Heavenly said. "I'm not a member of the family."

"I feel like you are," said Robby. "Don't you feel that way, Kit?"

"Yes," I said.

"How about you, Samara?" Robby asked. "Don't you feel like she's a member of the family?"

"Only if she wants to go back home," Samara said.

"No, kids," Heavenly said with a shake of her head. "I'm touched that you feel that way about me, but this is not my decision."

"So what is the decision?" I asked, turning to my parents and suddenly feeling nervous.

Mom looked at Dad. Dad looked at Mom. Then Mom looked at me. "I'm sorry, Kit. Before dinner your father and I agreed that we would move here only if all of the kids wanted it. Since two of you want to go home to Soundview Manor, I'm afraid that's what we're going to do."

Chapter

25

I felt like the *Titanic*, sinking in the ice-cold waters of the Atlantic Ocean. Go home? Leave Rafael? No! They couldn't be serious.

I stared across the table at Mom. She pursed her lips and gave me a sad look. Half of me wanted to argue, fight, and scream. The other half of me just wanted to cry.

That's the half that won.

Heavenly followed me to the bathroom.

"Can I help?" she asked while I dabbed my eyes with tissues.

"Can you make Chance and Samara want to stay?" I asked.

Heavenly thought for a moment, then shook her head.

"What about magic?" I whispered.

"It wouldn't be right," she whispered back.

"Why not?" I asked, a little desperate. "You could make them think they wanted to stay."

"No," Heavenly said. "I'm not supposed to interfere with their lives. If something goes wrong, I can make it right. But I'm not supposed to play God."

"But maybe they'd discover they really liked it here," I argued. "It might be the best thing in the world for them."

Heavenly gave me a crooked smile and put her hand on my shoulder. "I'm sorry, Kit. I can't. It's bad enough that you, Chance, and Robby know. Cocci would kill me if she found out. I think you guys know that I would never misuse my powers, but there are still many people who are fearful and ignorant. Cocci used to tell me over and over again that I had to be careful because if the wrong people found out, it could be very bad."

I nodded and sniffed and knew there was no sense in arguing. Heavenly was a good person, and she knew how I felt. If there'd been any way she could have helped me, I knew she would have.

The bathroom door opened and Mom stuck her head in. "You okay?"

I nodded and wiped my eyes.

"Can I help?" she asked.

"I'll be all right," I said. "Just give me a moment."

My family waited on the sidewalk outside the restaurant for me, and when I came out, they all gave me sad, sympathetic looks, as if they understood. Even Samara seemed to understand.

We started back to our hotel. Mom and I walked together.

"I'm sorry, hon," she said.

"It's not your fault," I said.

"I'm the reason you came to Italy," she said.

"That's not it," I said. "I should have been smarter. I should have known there'd be a good chance we weren't moving here."

Mom slid her arm around my waist. "You're growing up, and I never get to see it. All I do is work."

"I know you try to see us every chance you get," I said.

"I know," Mom said, "but I'm starting to feel that it's not enough."

There was a really good gelato place on the corner next to our hotel, and Dad suggested we all stop and get some.

"No, thanks," I said.

"Come on, hon, it'll make you feel better," Mom said.

"Sorry, but nothing's going to make me feel

better," I said. "You guys stay here. I'm just going to go up to my room."

I dragged myself down the sidewalk alone and into the hotel lobby. All I could think about was Rafael. I just wanted to see him so badly, but somehow I couldn't quite bring myself to go up to his room and bang on his door. He was probably out with his parents anyway.

I got into the lobby and started toward the elevator.

"Kit?"

I turned. Jessica was coming toward me from the reception desk. She was scowling.

"Oh, hi," I mumbled.

"Are you okay?" she asked. "Is something wrong?"

As you can probably imagine, Jessica was the last person in the world I wanted to tell my troubles to.

I gritted my teeth.

Forced a smile on my face.

And burst into tears.

Chapter

26

"T hat's so terrible," Jessica said. We were sitting on a couch behind a potted palm in a corner of the lobby where no one could see us. I'd just blurted out my whole miserable story to Jessica. Amazingly, she actually seemed to listen.

"Why don't you just stay?" she said.

I looked at her as if she was crazy. "Here in Rome? By myself?"

"Sure," she said. "Get your parents to find a family for you to live with. You can enroll in the American School here in Rome. Then on the weekends you can take the train up to Como to see Rafael, or he can take the train down here to see you."

I waited for her to wink or smile, but she looked perfectly serious.

"I . . . I couldn't do that," I said.

"Why not?" Jessica asked. "You're crazy about him, aren't you?"

"Yeah, but . . . not *that* crazy," I said.

Jessica smiled a little.

I was amazed to find that even though my eyes were still wet with tears, I was smiling back. She was right. It wasn't the end of the world.

It just *felt* like it was!

Chapter

27

You are going?" Rafael had a pained look on his face.

"Yes. In a few hours," I said.

We were holding hands, sitting on an ancient marble bench in front of a fountain in the Borghese gardens. Birds played in the fountain, and the leaves of the trees rustled slightly in the breeze. Rafael's parents were dragging his sister through the Villa Borghese.

Rafael squeezed my hand. "I am sorry to hear that."

"Me, too," I said.

A young mother pushing a baby stroller stopped to gaze into the fountain. Two teenage girls with black hair and bright red cell phones glued to their ears walked past, both chatting loudly on their phones. I tried to think of something to say to Rafael that didn't sound totally dumb and flaky.

"Maybe you will come back soon?" Rafael said.

"Maybe," I replied, although I sort of doubted it now that Mom had decided not to take the job.

"Maybe I will come to the United States," he said.

"I hope so," I said, although it was hard to believe that his parents would ever set foot on American soil voluntarily.

A butterfly fluttered past. It looked like a tiger swallowtail, but it was smaller and paler than the ones we saw back home. Rafael reached into his pocket and pulled out a pen. Then he started to look through his wallet.

"What are you looking for?" I asked.

"Something for write on," he said.

"Something *to* write on," I corrected him.

"Yes." Rafael shook his head. "The one time I am not bringing my sketch pad."

Suddenly he smiled and pulled a 1,000 lira note out of the wallet. He started to write on it.

"Wait!" I gasped. "That's money!"

"Is worth it," he said with a wink. I saw that he was writing down his address. When he was finished, he handed me the note.

"Thank you, Rafael," I said. Then I reached

into my own pocket. I had some lira notes and a few dollars. I took out one of the dollars and then borrowed Rafael's pen.

"Don't ever show this to anyone," I said as I wrote my name and address on the margin of the bill. "I'm not sure, but I think I could be arrested for doing this."

"I will never tell," he said with a wink.

"Ahem!"

At the sound of someone clearing his throat, we looked up and found Rafael's parents and sister standing before us. His parents had big frowns on their faces as they stared at the money we'd scribbled on. No doubt they were wondering what weird American custom led me to want to do something like that, and what a bad influence I was on Rafael for causing him to do it, too.

Rafael's mother spoke to him in harsh-sounding Italian, and even though I once again couldn't understand a word, I knew *exactly* what she was saying.

Rafael turned to me with a grim look on his face. I could see that he was having a hard time finding the words he wanted to say.

"I know," I said before he could speak, "it's time to go."

He nodded, then turned back to his parents and said something. His little sister grinned and his parents nodded and turned away.

"They will go away and wait for me," Rafael said.

A moment later his parents turned a corner. His little sister craned her neck to look at us one last time, and then disappeared.

Rafael moved close and took my face in his hands. I closed my eyes and felt his lips on mine. We shared a long, sweet, unhurried kiss.

My eyes were filled with tears when it ended. Rafael stroked my hair and studied me closely. Then he kissed me once more and said, *"Ciao,* Kit."

"Ciao, Rafael."

He stood up and started away. I sat on the bench. As he passed the fountain, I saw him reach into his pocket, pull out a coin, and toss it over his left shoulder without looking.

Plop! It made a little splash in the fountain.

And even though there were tears running down my cheeks, I had to smile.

Postscript

I spent most of the flight home writing Rafael a very long letter. Writing isn't one of my favorite activities, but at least it makes you feel a little closer to someone you can't be with.

After what seemed like forever, one of the flight attendants came on the speaker and said we were only an hour from landing. I closed my notebook then and gazed out the window at the thick blanket of white clouds below us.

I remember thinking, *You're going back to Soundview Manor, Kit. Back to the same old place and the same old life.*

Little did I know that very soon after the plane landed, everything would change. Not just for me and my family, but for Heavenly, too.

About the Author

TODD STRASSER has written many award-winning novels for young and teenage readers. Among his best-known books are those in the *Help! I'm Trapped In . . .* series. He has also written *Shark Bite, Grizzly Attack, Buzzard's Feast,* and *Gator Prey* in the *Against the Odds* series, published by Minstrel Books. Todd speaks frequently at schools about the craft of writing and conducts writing workshops for young people. He and his wife, children, and Labrador retriever live in a suburb of New York. Todd and his family enjoy boating, hiking, and mountain climbing.

You can learn more about Todd and the *Here Comes Heavenly* series at www.toddstrasser.com.

Jeff Gottesfeld and Cherie Bennett's

MIRROR IMAGE

When does a dream become a nightmare?
Find out in MIRROR IMAGE as a teenage girl
finds a glittering meteorite, places it under her pillow,
and awakens to discover that her greatest wish
has come true…

STRANGER IN THE MIRROR

Is gorgeous as great as it looks?

RICH GIRL IN THE MIRROR

Watch out what you wish for…

STAR IN THE MIRROR

Sometimes it's fun to play the part
of someone you're not
…until real life takes center stage.

FLIRT IN THE MIRROR

… From tongue-tied girl to the ultimate flirt queen.

From Archway Paperbacks

Published by Pocket Books

2312

Todd Strasser's

Here Comes Heavenly

Look for a new title every other month starting in
October 1999

Here Comes Heavenly

She just appeared out of nowhere. Spiky purple hair, tons of
earrings and rings. Hoops through her eyebrow and nostril,
and tattoos on both arms. She said her name was Heavenly
Litebody. Our Nanny. Nanny???

Dance Magic

Heavenly is cool and punk. She sure isn't the nanny our
parents wanted for my baby brother, Tyler. And what's with
all these ladybugs?

Pastabilities

Heavenly Litebody goes to Italy with the family and causes all
kinds of merriment! But...is the land of amore ready for her?

Spell Danger

Kit has to find a way to keep Heavenly Litebody, the Rand's
magical, mysterious nanny from leaving the family
forever.

Available from Archway Paperbacks
Published by Pocket Books

2307

*In time of tragedy,
a love that would not die...*

Hindenburg, 1937
By Cameron Dokey

San Francisco Earthquake, 1906
By Kathleen Duey

Chicago Fire, 1871
By Elizabeth Massie

Washington Avalanche, 1910
By Cameron Dokey

---

sweeping stories of star-crossed romance

Starting in July 1999

From Archway Paperbacks
Published by Pocket Books

2103